Apprentice to the Time Gods

Clark Graham

http:/facebook.com/elvenshore

elvenshore@gmail.com

See preview of A Witch's Revenge at the end of the book

Contents

Prologue

Red bricks of different hues formed the circle of the law house. The building stood three stories high, with a flat roof of timbers that overhung the bricks. It looked out of place in a town where people lived in huts and shopped in open-air markets.

Four guards stood in front of the large wooden doors. Uniformed in white pants and black shirts, they were armed with energy weapons. To Andri's mind, they had dour faces. His heart raced as his mother walked with him up to the men. His long, dark hair tossed in the slight wind.

"Stop." One of them held up his gloved hand.

"Here he is, you wanted him, take him." His mother wore a flowered dress she only used on special occasions. She sounded brave, but Andri could hear the shaking in her voice.

Two of the men stepped forward. Placing their hands on Andri's shoulder, escorted him forward. With a nod from one of them, the iron door was opened.

Andri had never been inside the building before. Neither had his father, nor his father before him. It was a place of judgment and deep discussion. Andri, at sixteen, had no need for either.

Torches illuminated the interior of the large room. Three rows of wood benches ringed around the solitary man in a white robe with a gold medallion around his neck. He stood in the center, leaning on his staff. "Bring the boy forward." The man motioned to the guards. Soon, Andri stood in the center of the room. "Here is Andri, question him yourselves." The guards walked back outside, closing the door behind them. It only served to make the dark room even darker.

Andri blinked in an effort to see better. Rel Li, the man next to Andri, had talked to him on several occasions. They had discussed Andri's willingness and how important to the planet, it was that

"Why were you chosen in place of a full-grown man?" A voice in the back spoke.

Rel Li pointed out to Andri the person who asked the question. All those sitting on the benches wore the same robes as Rel Li.

Andri shrugged. "It is not up to me to know the will or the thoughts of the Time Gods, nor why they would want someone like me to try and become one."

"Are you willing, for the sake of the planet, to do this?" another man asked.

Rel Li had explained many times how important becoming a Time God was to the planet. Andri would nod, but still not understand. His chances of even becoming a Time God were minimal. There were many men going to the trials. He was, by far, the youngest. *We are a strong race, compared to the others, and you are a strong boy amongst this race. You will be fine.* Rel Li's voice filled his memory.

Andri took a deep breath. "Yes."

"Will you keep the Tescires from invading us again?"

That's the whole of it, isn't it? He knew. That was the reason the planet had celebrated when they announced one of their own would be going to the trials. That lasted up until they found out Andri was only sixteen. Their joy turned to horror. It was as if the Time Gods, themselves, were mocking the people. You can be in the trials, but a boy is your only chance. To most, it wasn't much of a chance.

A fool's hope, his own mother had said, when she thought Andri was out of earshot. "I will do everything in my power to stop the Tescire from invading."

Cheers went up from all the delegates. They stood up and pounded on the benches in front of them. Rel Li held up his arms until they quieted down. "I will let Andri go and get ready. They will come for him soon. He turned to Andri. "I believe I speak for all of us when I say, I'm proud of you. All of our hopes and dreams go with you to your trials."

Andri gave him a bow. Rel Li whistled and the guards came down and escorted Andri out. "You should be honored. The council rarely brings anyone in to ask questions, except those who are worthy of death," the guard whispered.

Andri swallowed. *Worthy of death?* It didn't sound like a good thing. "Thank you." Andri said. When they exited the building, Andri ran home. His mother's open arms awaited him. "How did it go?"

"They asked me questions. They are worried I will fail, as is everyone else."

She ran her fingers through his black, unruly hair. "Do your best. There will be no shame if they know you gave it your best."

He nodded. "Yes, Momma."

"A package has arrived for you." She pointed over to his bed. "It's from the temple of the Time Gods."

Eagerly, he opened it. He frowned. "It's only clothes."

"Put them on. I will make sure they fit and take them in if needed."

He shrugged, and then did what she asked.

He wasn't ready to leave. His father lived in the same house as had his family for many generations. Andri had expected to live there, too, and raise a family when the time came. *What are my chances? I'll be back soon enough.*

His mother entered the room. She took her pins out and pinned the places she would need to take in. "They could have asked your size before they sent this." After she finished, she ran her hand through his hair again. "I do love you, son. You'll do well."

He smiled, but thought, *I hope not.*

Chapter One

The ball careened off the street and up against a nearby hut. The giggling child with disheveled hair and a patched sackcloth dress ran after it. She kicked it back onto the street where several boys put it back in play. The game came to an abrupt stop when a spacecraft appeared over the tree level.

One of the boys, rope tied around his waist to keep his raggedy pants from falling down, grabbed the ball to keep it from getting crushed, then ran to the side of the road.

Dirt kicked up as the powerful engines slowed the descent of the oval black ship. It touched lightly down on the dirt street. People came out of the huts to see it, but no one seemed too concerned. They had been expecting it. The doors opened from the side and a ramp set down. Out marched four tall men in red robes, their faces shaded by their hoods. Each had a long staff in their hand, straight, with the shape of the serpent's head on the top. The toc'fi was a crude weapon that released an electric charge when it touched someone. It could be set to kill. A fifth man followed. He wore solid black tunic and pants. The four red-robed men stopped in the center of the street. The black-clothed man stood in the middle of them.

"I am Keldore, guardian of the stone. We have come to collect Andri. Please bring him forward."

A grey-bearded man sporting a white robe walked up to the group, stopping just outside the reach of the toc'fi. "I am Rel Li, the leader of this people. The boy will be here in a few minutes."

Andri's mother put the finishing touches on Andri's new outfit. It was a black tunic with red trim, nicer fabric than had been seen in generations in the village. The clothes had been sent ahead. She brushed his shoulder, then kissed his cheek. Letting go a sob, she cried, "I'll never see you again."

He hugged her. "They are bringing men from all corners of the galaxy. I'm just one of many, and most of them will come back home."

She leaned back and put her hands on his shoulders. "I hope you're right." She gave him one last hug then let him depart out of the hut's door.

Andri walked up to Keldore. "I am ready."

The two pilots had exited the hovercraft and leaned against the hull. Their perfectly pressed uniforms were a stark contrast to the villagers around them. One whispered to the other, "He doesn't look much like a Time God to me."

"Silence!" Keldore hissed as he glared at them. The two pilots beat a hasty retreat back into the ship. Keldore turned back to Andri, with a softened expression, he said, "Come, your trials await."

Andri nodded and followed Keldore and the four red-robed keepers of the stone into the ship.

The door snapped shut behind him. Andri glanced around. Inside the ship was palatial compared to the huts of his village. Well-cushioned seats covered in crushed red velvet outlined the inside.

"Come sit," beckoned Keldore. "You have much to do after we arrive. You should rest."

Andri took a seat next to him. It was soft and comfortable and soon he had drifted off to sleep.

Andri woke up suddenly and sat up. Had it all been a dream? He half-expected to find himself in his own bed at home, pulling the worn blankets up to his chin. He turned to see Keldore sleeping beside him. The four keepers of the stone had taken off their robes and lounged around the seats in clothes much like the ones Andri wore. Three slept, one read from a pad. Andri could see out the front of the craft, stars whizzed by as they headed deeper into the galaxy. The two pilots were surrounded by displays and different colored lights and buttons, each man intent on the task at hand.

Keldore stretched, then gazed up. "Ah, you're awake." He stood up and looked out the front windows. "The Gadizza cluster. We're almost to your new home."

"How can you tell the difference between one star and another? They all look like dots in the sky that flash by as we race through space."

Keldore positioned Andri to a better vantage point. "See that circle of stars?"

Andri nodded.

"That is the six stars of the Gadizza cluster. In the center of those is the planet Gad, where the suns never set, but lights the planet on all sides."

"That must be really strange."

"It's a wonderful strange. You'll get used to it."

"How long do you think I'll last? I'm only sixteen. The others are much older than I. Why was I chosen?"

"Ah, the questions. I knew they would come eventually. I did not choose you; the Time Gods chose you.

Their wisdom is centuries older than mine. They have their reasons for choosing you, but they do not share those with me."

"Have you met the Time Gods?"

"No, only the one I met before he became one. I did not see him again afterward. Only once in a generation do the Time Gods call for the tests. You will be too old for the next rounds, so I suppose, this was your only chance to be one."

"It is an honor I do not want. I would have been happy growing up to be a farmer like my father and his father before him."

"The galaxy does need farmers, but it needs Time Gods more." Keldore smiled. The ship slowed down perceptively. "Wake up, keepers of the stone. We are almost there. It is time to don the robes and escort our guest to the altar."

The men lounging around the room, sprang to their feet. Each threw on a red robe and pulled up their hoods. Grabbing their toc fi's, they stood facing the door.

"Andri, you have the honor of standing in front of me as we go down the ramp. The keepers will walk on either side of us as we exit the ship."

Andri swallowed hard.

Chapter Two

The ship landed with a thunk. Keldare glared at the pilots when he regained his balance. With a sheepish smile, the one shrugged, "Sorry, the gravity on this planet is stronger than I'm used to." He pushed the button, and the door slid open.

The six of them walked down the ramp in formation as if they were on parade. Andri looked in wide-eyed wonder at the temple around him. It was like the castles he had read about as a boy. A tall rectangular wall surrounded them. It wasn't as wide as it was long. Andri could barely see the distant wall in front of him, blocked by a large tan brick open building with giant pillars supporting the roof.

Lining the sides were keepers attired in red robes, standing shoulder to shoulder, their toc'fi's pointing to the sky. Andri kept pace with the four keepers around him until they stopped in front of the tan building, nondescript except for its size. The building covered a huge rounded stone, half-buried in the ground.

A man stood in front of the stone. Andri's party walked up and stopped and faced him. On either side of the stone were men dressed identically to Andri, ten on one side, nine on the other. They were grown men, older and taller than Andri.

"Andri, I am Estran, the mouthpiece of the Time Gods. You will join your fellow trial members." Estran nodded in the direction of the nine. "Andri, will you please join them on the side of the stone. The trials will start in the morning." Keepers put a brown robe on each of the trial participants. "Keldare will show you to your quarters."

Keldare motioned to the group. "This way."

Following the others, Andri descended down a broad staircase, down the worn steps to a row of small apartments. A bed, a washbasin, barren otherwise, he took his place as indicated. Twenty identical apartments, ten on each side of the hallway. Each man was assigned to one. The apartments had no doors.

Andri sat down on his bunk. It had one blanket and was hard as a rock. *Keldare knew what he was talking about when he said to get some rest while I was on the ship.*

Two men stood in Andri's doorway. The taller one with brown hair and a permafrown, said, "See, I told you there was a mere boy among us." He laughed, the other one didn't.

"I'm Andri. What is your name?"

"Buliston, but you can call me 'Nightmare'. I'm the next Time God and no one can stand in my way." He walked inside and shoved Andri. "Do you understand?" He walked away without waiting for an answer.

"I'm Jak, I just met Buliston. I'm sorry, I didn't know what he was like until now." Walking up, Jak shook Andri's hand. He sat down on the bunk next to him. "Where are you from?" Jak set his hands in his lap. He had dark red hair and stood only two inches taller than Andri, but a good head below Buliston.

"I'm from the planet Malgado. I don't want to be a Time God. I was summoned and so I came. That's why I'm here."

"Malgado? No wonder it took so long for you to get here. We had to wait a day for you. Some of the others are from nearby planets, but most of us are from Gad."

Buliston walked back by the door, but stopped and backtracked. "Hey, Red. If you talk to children, then you're no friend of mine."

"My name is Jak, and I guess I'm no friend of yours then."

Buliston walked into the room. "Fine," he said as he punched Jak in the nose. "If you're no friend of mine, you're my enemy, along with the child. You won't like being my enemy, trust me." Then he left.

Jak's head reeled backward. He grabbed his nose. Blood seeped between his fingers. Andri rushed to the washbasin and handed Jak the washcloth. Jak held it over his nose. "You're not supposed to hit the other contestants."

"Could you get him banished for this?" Andri asked.

"I could, but now I want to beat him fair and square." Jak handed the washcloth back to Andri. He put it in the bowl, staining the water red.

The main door at the end of the hall squeaked shut. Turning the rooms black. "I've got to go." Jak groped his way out of the room and down the hall. Andri could barely see his outline as he crept away. *I guess it's time to sleep.* Andri sprawled on the hard mattress, his thoughts reeling.

The light streaming through the open door woke Andri hours later. He stood up and stretched to relieve the stiffness in his bones. Going to wash his face, he remembered the blood in the basin from Jak's nose. The water was clear. Someone had changed the water and the cloth while he slept. How had he not heard anyone in his room? He must have slept more soundly that he thought.

A half-hour later, the men stood around the stone. Andri wore the uniform and brown robe. He matched the others.

"Today is the first day of your trial. Stand fast." Estran said.

Twenty red-robed keepers walked up to the men. One keeper stood behind each contestant. Leaning their toc'fi's forward, they shocked the men in front of them.

Andri gasped, gritting his teeth against the pain. One man screamed. He was led away by the keeper behind him. Seeing the keepers turning up the power level of their toc'fis, Andri braced for the next jolt. It wasn't long in coming. A sharp pain started in his back, shot up his arms and down his legs. He shivered but stood fast. Two men dropped to their knees. They were both led away.

Again, the keepers raised the power level. Andri felt the toc'fi against his back again. He clenched his fist and gritted his teeth again, waiting for the next jolt. When it came, it took his breath away. He shook violently and gasped for air. His knees buckled, but he didn't fall. Regaining his composure, he inhaled. Every part of his being tingled, and his ears were ringing.

Four men fainted from the pain; they were taken away.

"That is enough for today. Take them back to their rooms," Estran said.

Keldore showed the men the way. Some limped as they walked, but Andri wanted them to know he wasn't defeated. He held his head up high as he made his way down the stairs.

Estran strolled over and stood at Aladar's side, her long, sleek figure outlined in the form-fitting dress. She flipped her shoulder-length black hair behind her as she leaned in. "Yes, what is it?"

"I thought the boy would fail this first day, but he's still here. Why would the Time Gods choose someone so young, Mistress of the temple?"

"We cannot say what the Time Gods are thinking, but I do know the boy is from the race of Belldestar from the planet Malgado. Warrior blood flows through his veins. They were attacked in the valley of Sandrall by a force of Tescire. Ten thousand Bellldestar against five times that many Tescire. The Belldestar held their ground. Fifty thousand more Tescire came with heavy weapons. Outmanned and outgunned, the Belldestar fought on. They were wiped out, to a man, but the Tescire lost twice as many men, and eventually the war." She turned to face Estran. "That is the heritage of the boy."

"Isn't Buliston a Tescire?"

"Yes, but you mustn't tell Andri. Hate still runs deep. The Tescire tried to take Andri's planet by force. No Tescire has ever dared ventured to near the race of Belldestar since then."

Estran nodded.

Chapter Three

Jak sat on Andri's bunk with his back to him. "Yes, it's bad. Three intersecting circles, each one redder as they go up your spine. At least my keeper hit me in the same place all three times."

Jak slipped his shirt back on. "That would have hurt worse, I think."

"I don't know, it all hurt terribly."

"Yeah, it did. Have you seen Buliston? Someone said he was holed up in his room."

"I don't care about him. If he holed up in his room the rest of the time, it would be okay with me."

Jak shook his head. "He tried to befriend me the first day. I think the others knew what he was like and gave him a wide berth. I didn't know him, but before you know it, he's punching me in the nose."

"I still think you should have reported it. He would have been gone already."

Jak laughed, "And miss out on seeing him suffer with the rest of us? Not a chance."

"I guess you're right, why should we suffer alone?"

Women with platters full of food came down the stairs. Each man was handed a plate. Steak, steaming vegetables, and a mug of ale graced each plate. "Smells great." Jak said as he sat down on the bunk to eat.

Andri set the ale aside and started in on his steak.

"You're not going to drink that?" Jak asked." Can I have it?"

"Sure," Andri replied as he handed the drink over to Jak.

"Great, I love this stuff. Nice and strong, it takes the edge off the pain."

"It also takes the edge off your senses."

"My senses don't need an edge tonight," Jak took a drink.

The lights went out a few hours later. Andri lay in the dark, staring at a ceiling he could barely see. *Why am I here? I could be in my bed back home.* He thought of his mother. *Will I ever see her again?*

"Don't despair, young Andri, the Time Gods have a reason for everything they do."

He looked up to see the outline of a woman in his doorway. "Who are you?"

"A friend for the time when you lose all your other friends." The woman walked away.

He stood up to follow her, but she wasn't in the dark hallway. He returned to his bunk and fell into a fitful sleep.

The door opened in the morning and the initiates filed out to stand next to the rock in their brown robes.

A woman stood forth. "I am Aladar, the mistress of the temple. Another of your companions has quit your ranks during the night. There are only twelve of you left. Congratulations on making it this far."

That's her. He stared up at Aladar. She locked eyes for a second and smiled, then resumed speaking.

"Today you will have a big breakfast before your trial."

The same women as the night before brought out platters of eggs and fried meats. Large plates and glasses were also provided. He poured himself a glass of milk and grabbed some eggs and meat. He was about to dig in when he realized he had no idea what would be required of him today, so he ate only half of his breakfast.

Jak leaned back, rubbing his stomach, "I'm so full. That was such a great meal."

"Line up along the back of the temple," Estran ordered. The men complied. "You will run to the far wall and back to here. You may take off your robes for this trial." When they did so Estrian said, "Go."

Andri took off quickly and soon outpaced the rest of the pack. He touched the back wall and turned to make his way back to the temple. Buliston ran into him and knocked him over. Andri stood up, but by this time, Buliston had turned the corner. He shoved Andri down again. Regaining his feet, Andri ran harder, just catching up with the rest of the pack as they reached the temple. Three stragglers came in after him. Keepers led the stragglers away from the temple of the stone.

Jak made his way to the side, away from the temple then vomited out his breakfast. Looking up, he half expected to see a keeper walk him out of the temple grounds, but none came.

Back down the stairs he lay in his bunk, moaning.

"What's the matter?" Andri asked as he stood in Jak's doorway.

"That was such a good meal and I puked it out. My stomach hurts."

"Hang in there, we have to stick together. It's us against Buliston."

Jak sat up. "I saw what he did. You were winning. What a cheater"

"In the end, it didn't matter. I'm still here despite his best efforts."

Aladar stood at the edge of the temple staring into space. Estran came up to him. "Are you talking to the Time Gods?"

"Not talking, listening to what they have to say."

"Do they tell you to send Buliston home? He cheated today. The Time Gods hate a cheater. He will never be one of them now."

Aladar shook her head. "No, Buliston will stay. He will never be a Time God, but his gift is adversity, and that will help the next Time God grow."

"I see," he smiled. "That tells me more than you intended to."

"Does it? Or are you reading too much into this?"

"Now you're trying to confuse me. I don't confuse easily."

Chapter Four

Buliston stood in Andri's doorway, fist clenched, fire in his eyes. "You are going to lose today, one way or another. If you don't give up, I'll beat you when I get back."

Andri stood his ground calmly. "Why wait? If you want to beat me, do it now."

Buliston took two steps toward Andri.

"Breakfast is served," came Aladar's now familiar voice. A dozen women walked down the hall with platters of food. "And just in time, it seems."

She eyed Buliston as he turned on his heel and left Andri's quarters.

Placing a platter on Andri's bed she said, "Watch out for that one."

"I do not fear him."

She smiled, "I know. There isn't anything that you fear except becoming a Time God." The other women were making their way up the steps. She followed.

When the men were lined up, each keeper tied the candidate's hands were tied behind his back. Facing a table, long knives were placed in front of them.

Estran raised his hand and said, "Go."

Andri turned his back to the table and managed to turn the knife, edge up, using his fingertips. He sawed off the ropes and raised his hand well before the others.

Buliston had picked up the knife but struggled to cut the cords with it. Still, he did somehow. He slid the knife under his robe when he was done. Jak dropped his knife on the ground and went down on his knees to try and retrieve it.

"Time is up," Estran called out. Only six of the contestants had managed to cut their bonds.

Jak sat down in a dejected heap on the ground, arms still tied behind his back. A keeper took pity on him and cut his ropes.

"Tonight, we will have the Feast of Ascension and in the morning one of you will become a Time God," Estran said. All the keepers bowed to the six contestants who were left.

Andri went back down to his room, half expecting Buliston to already be there. Instead, Jak sat on this bed, his looked down at the ground. "I failed today. I wish you the best of luck in the morning, I hope the Time Gods will pick you."

"He won't live to see the dawn."

Buliston stood in the doorway, brandishing the knife.

"You can't do this," Jak tried to get between the two but Buliston backhanded him, sending him face-first onto the bed.

"If you're going to stab me, aim well." Andri stood tall. "You will only get one chance."

Buliston lunged forward, thrusting the knife in Andri's direction. Andri sidestepped it, bringing his elbow full force onto Buliston's wrist. The knife slid across the floor. Twisting his body, Andri kicked Buliston's legs out from under him. He landed with a thud, knocking the wind out of him.

Buliston's shirt rode up, revealing the tattoo of a Tescire warrior. Andri's face reddened. He picked up the knife and stepped forward. Hovering over Buliston's prone figure, still struggling for breath, Andri stood there for a minute. "No, I won't kill you, although you deserve to die. Get out of my room." He stuck the knife in the wall.

Buliston regained his feet, then retreated out of the room.

Estan strolled up to Aladar, "There is a fight in the downstairs rooms. Should you not go down and see what it is?"

"I know what the commotion is." Aladar slowly shook her head. "There is no need for me to go down there."

"So, what is this commotion then?"

"It's the next Time God passing his final test."

The remaining men were called upstairs that evening. Tables were set up along the edges of the temple, surrounding the stone. Andri had never seen this much food in his life. He didn't even know what most of it was. One of the remaining candidates sat at the head of each table. When Buliston went to sit down, two keepers grabbed his arms, holding him fast.

Estran walked over to him. "You have disgraced this contest with your mere presence. You will depart, never to step on this holy ground again." He turned to the keepers, "Take him away."

When Andri sat down, he gazed over to see Estran sitting at his left hand.

"Well, Andri, you were the youngest, yet you're still here. I underestimated you."

"I'm as surprised as you are."

A tray full of different meats was brought over to him. Andri stared at it for a moment, not knowing what to do.

"Try the wild boar," Estran whispered. "It's from Zeldanar and has a rich and robust flavor."

"Which one is that?" he whispered back.

"The dark meat in the middle."

He pointed at it and the server placed it on his plate. "Thank you," he said to Estran.

Several more trays were brought, and the same patterned played out. Soon Andri had a heaping plate full of food. "I can't eat all this," Andri complained.

"You're not expected to. Try a little of each, then you'll know what to take next time."

"It was a sin to waste food where I came from. We never knew if there would be enough to hold us over the winter."

"Maybe we're spoiled living on this planet. There is no winter here. The crops grow year-round so there is always food. We are the king of the feasts."

Andri furrowed his brow. "Do the Time Gods have feasts like this?"

He shrugged, "Only Aladar can answer that question, and she won't. 'The less you know about Time Gods,' she says, 'the better off you'll be.'"

Andri looked around the grounds. "One of us will soon find out." He looked again, "Where's Buliston?"

"He isn't worthy of the honors that will be bestowed on the rest of you. He had to leave. You will never see him again."

Andrie breathed a sigh of relief, then tasted the wild boar. "It's good."

This left Estran wondering if it was the boar that was good, or never seeing Buliston again was good, or both.

Chapter Five

The five contestants were awakened early the next morning, fed, and brought up to the temple with their brown robes on. A crowd had gathered inside the gate. People spoke in hushed voices.

Andri's heart raced. He had never seen so many people in his entire life. The fear of the unknown was also upon him.

"Place your hands on the stone," Estran ordered.

The five men complied. Keepers stepped forward and blindfolded the five.

"Now is the time has come. Take off your blindfolds."

When the men complied. "Take off the brown robes of the contestants and put the red robes of the keepers on these four."

The four stepped back, looking at each other and around the temple, until they realized, Andri was no longer there. They donned the robes, then joined the rank of the keepers.

His hand on the stone, Andri fell forward when the cold stone of the rock suddenly became liquid. He grabbed at something, anything to break his fall, but found nothing solid. He landed, shoulder first, on a flat sandy surface.

He strained to see his surroundings, but the inky darkness enveloped him. Standing, he reached out to see what he could feel. When he stepped forward, he found a wall, a curved wall, smooth to the touch.

A flicker of a yellowish light appeared to the side of
him. He watched it glow ever brighter. *A passageway?*
Someone is coming. He braced himself for the unexpected,
but then someone bearing two torches turned the corner.

"Aladar!"

"You sound surprised. I am the mistress of the
Temple. I brought you a torch to light your way. You will
take this passageway." She held the torch to the entrance.
"It is a place I will not enter. It has been an honor to meet
you, Time God." She bowed, handed him a torch, then
made her way up the passageway she had come down.

Time God? She called me Time God. What does that
even mean? Taking a deep breath, he walked down the
other passageway. The gentle downward slope soon
became stairs that seemed to go on forever. He finally
arrived at the bottom where it flattened out. Red flickering
light illuminated the entrance to a cavern. He hesitated, but
only a moment, before stepping through.

There were red flames that erupted, then calmed
back down only to erupt again, in each corner of the room.
A large pool of water lay in the center. It was held in by
stones, waist high to Andri. The pool was perfectly still.
When Andri looked closer, he could see images moving
about, reflecting off the surface of the pool. It would show
a scene, then flash to another one, over and over again.
Andri stared, mesmerized by what he was seeing.

"The seer pool," came a voice behind him. Andri
whirled around to see a tall man standing there. He was
dressed simply in shirt and pants. Sandals adorned his feet.
His hair was gray and shoulder length. "It shows all the

travelers and what they are doing. Welcome young Andri.
We have waited far too long for you."

"Waited for me? I barely finished the competition."
His head spun. "What's a traveler?"

"First things first. Augustin is my name. We do not
call ourselves Time Gods. That's Aladar's name for us. We
call ourselves travelers. Another one of Aladar's inventions
is the competition. You would have won, no matter what.
She included Buliston the Tescire as an added test, but you
were selected the day you were born to become one of us.
We have always been mindful of you. We took you at an
early age, because there are things you can do that the older
men can't. Enough of that. I will show you to your quarters.
Follow me."

Augustin led him around the pool. to the far end of
the chamber. Two metal doors opened as if by magic and
Andri gasped.

"Coming from your world, it will take some time to
become familiar with our technology, but you will quickly
catch on. I, too, had a hard time with it at first. I came from
a backward planet like you did."

As they entered the doorway, Andri heard a
splashing sound behind him. He turned to see someone
walking out of the seer pool. The man was tall with straight
brown hair and a crooked smile.

"Trevor, this is Andri. He's finally here."

Trevor stood in front of him and bowed. "It is a
pleasure to meet you." Then he smiled at Augustin. "You
said, *finally* here. Andri, time has no meaning for us."

"I was putting it into terms Andri would understand.
He is correct. Time has no meaning. We do not know when

we go forward or backward in time. All we care about is the mission."

"What mission?" Andri asked.

"That is up Aladar and the seer pool. She sends us in, and she determines where and when we come out. When we succeed, or fail, for that fact. She brings us back."

"You can fail? Where do you go?" Andri's mind reeled. "You're not wet; how could you have come out of the water dry?"

Augustin raised his hand. "So many questions. The answers will come another day. For today, we relax. Andri, you are now an apprentice to the travelers. When you are ready, you will enter the seer pool. For now, you rest and learn. You have much to know before the seer pool calls you."

"I'm sorry. I'm eager to know what lies ahead for me."

"It's good to ask questions, but the answers will come in your training. Do not worry, you'll know everything by the end," Trevor responded.

As the three of them entered through the doorway, lights came on and illuminated a long white hallway. Everything was perfectly square, unlike the mud buildings of Andri's home.

"What is this place?" he asked in hushed tones.

"This is our home," responded Augustin. He stood in front of one of the side doors. "This is your room. Say, 'enter.'"

"Enter." The door opened with a swoosh. "Wow." He gazed around the room. It was twice the size of the chief elder's hut at home, and full of books. The bed was the largest he'd ever seen, and there was a sink and a bathroom built in. "This is incredible."

"You will study books. When you have enough knowledge, the seer pool will call. It is up to her. Don't ask us when that will be. We don't know."

Andri nodded. The two men bowed and left. Andri turned to admire his new home/chamber and said, "Wow," again.

Chapter Six

The evening had been spent eating and talking to the other travelers in the common room. Trevor called it the cafeteria, but they did other things than eat there. The food was an odd assortment of samples from the planets the travelers visited or were from. The travelers talked about their latest adventures and how long it would take before Andri would join them.

Some predicted months, the older ones predicted a year or two. That is how long their course of study had taken. Andri listened, totally enthralled at the Time Gods' stories. *They will always be Time Gods to me.* He didn't, for one second, like the term travelers. They talked about time like it existed. It measured days and weeks, but the time under the temple didn't match the time in the rest of the galaxy. A day of their time could be a year or two to everyone one else.

That night he settled into his quarters. Both his body and spirit were full. His major accomplishment, though, was figuring out the door. When he said 'enter' while inside, it wouldn't open. He had to use the word 'exit.' When saying 'exit' outside, it wouldn't work either. He finally found the word 'open' worked for both entering and exiting.

He lay down on his bed and said, "Dim lights ninety percent." The lights went down.

He had barely drifted off to sleep when a voice called his name.

"Andri."

Andri looked through the dim lights but couldn't see where the voice came from. 'Lights on full.' The room lit up. He walked around, but there was no one there.

"Andri."

The woman's voice seemed to come from beyond the door.

"Open." Walking out into the hall, he looked up and down but there was no one there.

"Andri, come here." The voice was calm, unrushed.

He walked towards the sound. The large metal doors to the seer pool opened as he approached. He saw a reflection in the waters. "Aladar, what are you doing here?"

"I'm the mistress of the temple, it is I who have the crystal that looks into the galaxies. I will not enter the seer pool, but my reflection does. I am the one who assigns the missions to the Time Gods. Enter the pool, Andri. I have an assignment for you. It's on a planet near the rim of the galaxy, the Orion's Arm, far away from the center, where we live."

"I'm not ready to enter the pool. The others have said so. I have much to learn before I do."

A soft laugh filled the space. "You will learn infinitely more by doing a task rather than reading about it. Come, enter the pool."

He took a deep breath and walked up the steps that led to the edge of the pool. Stepping in, he noticed it wasn't water, but a thicker substance.

"All the way in," Aladar urged.

He nodded and walked down the steps inside the pool. When he was neck-deep, he ducked his head under.

It's hot. Hotter than Andri ever remembered being. He wiped the sweat off his forehead. He looked down at his dirt-stained hand. Around him were white and black people. The planet Rojus had a warrior race who were black. Those were the only black people he'd ever seen. Looking down, his bare feet contrasted with the red soil.

"What are you doing there, child?" Andri turned to respond to find a white man, uniformed, in some sort of a vehicle. Instead of hovering, its round wheels touched the ground. There was some type of sign on the door in with the words Macon County Sheriff on it. *Everything is so strange.*

"I said, what you doing there, child? Where are your parents?" The man exited the vehicle, spitting something brown on the ground when he did. The man stood six feet high, his belly protruding over his belt. He had a weapon strapped to it.

"I'm just standing here."

"What's your name, child?"

"Andri."

"What are you doing at the edge of town all alone?"

Andri shrugged.

The man leaned over and pulled a handset from his car. "I think I found the runaway, Flo. I'll bring him in and see if this is the one."

"Thank you, Sheriff," came the reply.

"If you'll hop in my car here, son, I'll take you back to the orphanage where you belong." It wasn't an option. The sheriff grasped his arm and led him to the car, putting him in the back none too gently. "You've got Miss Flo all upset with worry, child."

They drove through down a road with two-story buildings of different shapes on sizes on either side. Finally arriving at a sparsely populated part of the town, the sheriff turned onto a dirt road. Andri bounced around in the backseat while the sheriff drove over the ill-kept road, they arrived at a large white house surrounded by slash pines. He escorted Andri into the front door up to a broad desk presided over by a white woman with a blue plaid scarf tied around her hair. She smiled when the sheriff came in, revealing her yellowed teeth.

"Here he is, Flo. Is this the one? He says his name is Andy."

"Andy? What an imagination. He always has been a joker. Come on, Anton. We'll take you back up to your room. John is really going to take a licken' to you for runnin off like that."

The sheriff tipped his hat on his way to the door. "Glad I could be of service." He walked back to his car.

A black woman wearing a grease-stained apron came out from the kitchen and scowled at Flo. "That ain't Anton. You know that ain't Anton. Your stealin' a child from its loving home. You can't do that."

"Now, Miss Emily, I run this house. This child is better off here anyway. Probably starvin' to death at that run-down shantytown east of here. At least he'll get three meals a day. Besides, the county gives us thirty dollars every month for each child. Now if they come in and Anton is missing, then that's less money to pay you with, isn't it? Besides, the sheriff brought him to us. It's all legal."

"This is wrong, Miss Flo."

Flo put her hands on her hips. "I pay you to cook, not to argue with me. Get back at it." She pointed to the kitchen.

Emily turned on her heels, muttering, "It ain't right."

"Don't mind her. Come, child, I'll show you to your room." They walked up the old stairway. Faded carpet tacked to each step, but the structure of them was solid wood. At the top of the stairs, they turned to the left. The room was about a quarter of the size of Andri's quarters at the seer pool. Four bunk beds took up most of the space. A box at the end of the bed held well-worn clothes.

"See if you can fit into Anton's clothes. If so, well, he won't have nothin' when he gets back, but oh, well, that'll teach him for running off like he did. The bunk on the top is yours." Flo walked out of the room.

Andri looked out the dirty window and saw kids playing tag in the field below. He marveled that, even across the galaxy, children came up with the same games. *Do Time Gods play tag?* He wanted to join them but thought better of it.

Flo sat back at her desk when John walked in. He removed his weather-stained grey hat and ran his hand through a shock of brown hair. He had a two-day stubble of a beard on his face and a leather cord wrapped around his hand. "I hear the sheriff was here. If he brought Anton back, I'll beat that boy black and blue. Where is he?"

"Just relax, John. He ain't here. The sheriff brought a boy, but it wasn't Anton."

John cocked his head. "Who is it, then?"

"His name is Andy. We'll call him Anton until the inspection is over, then we can call him what we want."

"But, does he have papers? Is he an orphan? What if the real Anton comes back?"

"Just relax, none of that matters. If Anton comes back, then we create papers for the new boy, and we'll get another thirty every month. The sheriff brought him. It's not our fault."

A slow smile spread across John's face. "Good thinking."

Chapter Seven

That night when the children gathered at the supper table, all the kids stared at Andri. He pulled out a chair, averting his gaze.

"What's his name?" asked one of them.

"You can call him Anton for now," Flo responded. "Now eat your dinner."

When Emily, the cook, placed a plate in front of Andri, he noticed his portions were just that much larger than everyone else's. He quickly took a few bites so none of the others would notice.

With dinner over, Flo sat back. "Well, children, who do you think should help Miss Emily clean up today?" In unison all the kids pointed at Andri.

"It's settled, then. The rest of you can go out and play."

Andri headed into the kitchen.

"Can you wash dishes, child?" Emily asked.

"Yes, Ma'am. My mother taught me."

"Where is your mother?" Emily stood back and put her hands on her hips. "Is she still alive?"

"Yes, as far as I know. My father too, but they are on a planet far away from here."

She let go of a laugh. "You're a space traveler, are you?"

"You don't travel to other planets?"

"No, of course not, and you don't neither. She lives on another planet, you say." She shook her head. "You don't be telling anybody about your space travel or you'll be in the mental house, not in the orphanage."

Andri was elbow deep in dishwater and scrubbing away. "I'm sorry. I didn't know."

"You talk like a northerner, not a Martian. Where you from anyway, child?"

"From a small village. Is it bad to be a northerner?"

"It is around here. Miss Bee from the county, she hates northerners. Don't talk while she's here. We'll all be better off that way. You must be from one of those shantytowns, Miss Flo talked about. She says you were starving.' You don't look like you starvin' to me."

"My father's a farmer. We had plenty to eat."

"I can get you out of here and back to your family." Emily stepped closer to Andri, her voice low. "I helped Anton escape. He's living with his uncle in Atlanta now."

"I can't leave. I haven't finished my mission yet. When I do, I'll be taken back."

"You talk in riddles, child. What mission would that be?"

He shrugged, "I don't know yet."

"What am I to do with you, space traveler?"

He washed off his hands after stacking the dishes.

"Go on," Emily said, "you done here. Go play with the kids."

Andri walked out on the red dirt playfield. The children were playing tag again. "Can I join in?"

"You're too old," one of the girls said, as she ran by.

He sat on a rock and observed. Although poor, the kids had better clothes than he wore growing up. His thoughts were brought back to his own childhood and the

small village. They had all been farmers and lived simply.
The huts and buildings were made of mud. At one time,
he'd heard, their planet had been an advanced, prosperous
society, but this only caused jealousy from other planets.
They wanted to take what his planet had. Many wars later,
their leaders realized, if they had nothing, then they had
nothing to lose. They gave up their advanced technology
and lived off the land.

"Hi."

Andri hadn't seen another boy come up and sit
down beside him. "Hi," he responded back.

"You're the new Anton, right?"

"No, my name is Andri. Miss Flo calls me Anton
because the county is coming in a few days to do a head
check and Anton is missing."

"He ain't missing, he done runned off. He ain't
never coming back."

Andri nodded. "What's your name?"

"Elijah, like in the Bible." He watched two kids
running by. "They say I'm too old to play their game, too."

Andri's brow furrowed, "The Bible, what's that?"

"You ain't never heard of the Good Book?"

Andri shook his head.

"Everyone believes in the Bible."

"Have you ever read it?"

"Nah, I ain't. My momma used to read it to me
every night though, until she passed. Pappa runned off long
before that, so they stuck me here. How about you, why's
you here?"

"I don't know yet. I was sent here to help, but I
don't know what that means." He stared straight ahead.

"You'll find your way. We all do eventually."

That night, Andri snuggled down to sleep. Suddenly he heard a scream coming from the woods. He leaped out of bed and pulled his pants on. He almost made it to the door when Elijah grabbed him from behind.

"Don't you never mind what's happenin' in them woods."

"Someone's being hurt."

"Yep, and you will be, too, if you go out there. When Mr. John gets his strap out, he's meanin' to use it." Elijah pulled at his arm. "Go back to bed. Ain't nothing good gonna happen if you go out there."

Another high-pitched yell, then sobbing, came from outside. Andri pulled his arm free. "I have to go."

Elijah pointed at the window. "It's all over now, anyways. See, there's John's coming back."

Going over to the window, Andri saw the same girl that had told him he was too old to play tag, coming out of the woods behind John. Even in the darkness he could see her holding her bottom. "Why would he do that?"

"Lisa tends to take other's things. She be thinking twice about it next time."

"The punishment doesn't fit the crime."

"You do talk like someone who ain't around here. Where you from?"

Andri listened to the front door close. Timid steps came up the stairs. "I'm from far away. Very far away."

Chapter Eight

Andri crawled back into bed, but he didn't sleep. He fumed. *He beat that child with a strap. How old is she, maybe ten?*

In the morning, after breakfast, he took Elijah to the side. "How many kids does John beat and why?"

"All of us been beat at one time or another. John, he's crazy. Germans captured him in the war and hurt him. Sometimes, when he gets really bad, you hear him screamin' during the night. Miss Flo, she has to go in and wake him."

When the children went out to play, Andri spotted the girl from last night. Sitting down next to her, he said, "I heard you yelling in the woods. Are you all right?"

"No, he hurt me bad." She held up her hands, red and swollen. "He whipped my backside and when I tried to cover it, he whipped my hands, too. I didn't steal nothin'. Miss Flo has pretty earrings, so I picked one up to look at it. I ain't never had nothing pretty in my life. I was just peekin'. She found me in her room and called me a thief. That's when she called Crazy John." She leaned against Andri and sobbed softly.

"Don't be helping that thief." Flo glared at them with her hands on her hips.

"She didn't take anything. She was just looking," Andri replied.

"You don't talk back to me, child."

The girl disappeared around the other side of the building. Andri stood up. "You're not my mother."

Elijah ran up to him and pulled him to the side. "Don't be sassin' Miss Flo. She'll send John after you and he'll beat you for sure."

"I'm not afraid of them. Their only power is fear. If you don't fear them, they have no power."

Elijah straightened up, eyes wide. "I ain't ever thought about that."

John came out the front door, pointing at Andri, "You better mind your manners around Miss Flo, child."

Andri folded his arms, "Or what?"

"Well, you best just mind your manners, hear?" John walked back into the house.

"Did you talk to him?" Flo asked.

"Yep, he'll never do it again."

"He'd better not or he'll get a visit to the woods."

"That little girl howled last night. I felt so bad."

She glared at him. "Your job is to discipline these creatures. There's no reason for you to be around if you don't do your job." She turned on her heel.

The next morning all the children were lined up in front of the building. Flo wasn't wearing her usual blue scarf. She had her hair in a bun with a pencil through it, instead. A big black car drove up and stopped in front of the orphanage.

Elijah leaned over and whispered to Andri, "Wow, a Packard."

"Is that a type of car?"

"Yep, a fancy one. It's Miss Emm's, only she don't drive it. I'm gonna have me one of those when I grow up, only I'll drive it my own self."

An older, heavy-set woman stepped out of the back seat. She wore a wide-brimmed hat with flowers on it. Grasping a battered clipboard, she walked up to the line of children.

"Hello, Miss Emm," they all said in unison, except for Andri.

"Well, thank you." Grabbing a pencil, she began reading off names then checking them off her list when they answered, "Here."

"Anton Morris." When no one answered she looked up from her list.

Flo nudged Andri.

"Anton Morris," Emm repeated.

"He's right here." Flo said, pointing, red-faced.

"I need him to answer."

"I'm not Anton. My name is Andri," he replied firmly. "The sheriff picked me up at the edge of town thinking I was Anton, and Miss Flo, she told me to lie to you."

"He's such a kidder and the silly name he's made up, Andri, no one's ever been named that. Tell her the truth, Anton." Flo hit him in the back of the head.

Emm shook her head. "Kids these days, and a northerner besides," then continued down the list. When she finished, she asked, "Everything going well?"

Flo smiled, "Wonderful."

"Glad to hear it." Emm walked back to her car and soon it was speeding off.

"John," Flo yelled. "John, I need you, now."

John staggered out of the front door. His eyes were blood-shot. He cinched up his belt as he walked.

"This boy here," she pointed to Andri, "don't do what he's told. Nearly got us in trouble. Go get your strap."

John grumbled as he headed back into the house. He came out with it wrapped around his fist. "Come with me, child." He grabbed Andri by the arm and led him into the woods.

"You can't whip him for tellin' the truth." Elijah flew in Flo's face.

"You go back into the house, child, or you'll be next."

"He done told the truth. He ain't done nothin' wrong."

"I said, get back in the house and mind your own business."

"But he ain't done nothin' wrong."

Andri turned to face John when they were in the woods.

"Turn around, or I'll aim for your face."

"I do not fear you."

"I'll teach you to fear," John unwound the strap and swung it at Andri's head.

Andri caught the end of the strap, pulled it out of John's hand, throwing it on the ground.

"How dare you?" John clenched his fists and lunged at Andri.

Andri sidestepped him. John turned and rushed again. Andri struck him square on the nose. John stopped in his tracks, took two stunned steps back and sat down, holding his nose.

"Ow." John looked at his hand. Blood dripped from his palm, so he put it back on his nose. "You broke it."

"You will never beat another child with that strap of yours." Andri stood over him, arms folded.

John looked up and nodded.

Andri walked out of the woods, not toward the house, but away from it. John headed towards the house, blood dripping down on the front of his shirt.

"What happened to you?" Flo asked. She was holding Elijah by the arm.

"I hit my nose on a tree."

"Never mind that." She pushed Elijah towards him. "This one's next."

John led the boy into the woods. The strap still lay on the ground.

Andri appeared at the side of a tree, behind's Elijah's back. John could see him and touched his nose instinctively. Then turned to Elijah. "You're gonna holler like I hit you real hard, you hear me? Then go running to the house and up to your room."

Elijah yelled and ran back towards the house.

Andri nodded, satisfied, and turned toward the dusty road. The air around him became thicker and thicker. The next thing he knew, his head exited the seer pool as he walked up the steps and down onto dry floor. He rubbed his hands. How was he dry?

Aladar's reflection appeared in the pool. "You did well, Time God. Elijah didn't ever get beaten again. He grew up to be a politician who helped lift orphans out of poverty. John would have beaten a child to death and be put in prison, if not for you. He learned other methods of discipline, and in the end, got over his nightmares and became the administrator of the orphan's home. Flo was fired for cheating on the books, and he wouldn't lie for her."

"And the little girl?"

"She became a mother of five, all of whom finished college. Now she has lots of pretty things of her own."

Andri scanned the room. "I expected some of the others to greet me when I came back."

"You have only been gone a few minutes of our time. They don't know you were on a mission. They want so much to prepare you. If you choose, you don't have to tell them."

Andri nodded. He slipped down the hallway and into his room.

A few minutes later, the bell on his door rang. "Open," he said.

Three of the travelers came into the room. One brought a small cake. "We thought we would explain missions to you, so you'll know what to expect."

Andri smiled, "Yes, that would be very interesting."

Chapter Nine

At breakfast the next morning, Andri sat across from Trevor. His long legs stretched all the way under the table, cramping Andri's space. Trevor leaned back in his chair, examining an egg.

"Can you reel in a little? I have no room for my feet."

"Oh, sorry." Trevor sat up. "I do take up space." His bright white teeth flashed an apologetic smile. "Did you know this egg comes from Elderas? It is from the rare Torkas bird and is a delicacy on forty-nine planets that don't even have Torkas birds. It's highly valued. Whenever Augustin visits one of those planets, he brings me an egg."

"That's good of him," Andri responded as he tasted his soup.

"The only problem is, I don't like them, and I don't know how to break the news to him."

Andri giggled. "That is a problem."

Augustin walked up. "Something's brewing, I think you're going to be called up soon, Andri. I can feel it."

"What makes you say that?" Andri responded.

"You are the only one in your age bracket. I'm surprised you haven't been called up yet."

"Well, as a matter of fact…"

"Trevor, you haven't eaten the egg yet?"

"Oh, no. One doesn't simply gobble down a Torkas egg. They must be examined first. The anticipation of the flavors is enhanced by waiting."

Andri hid his grin.

"Andri," Aladar's voice echoed through the room.

"I knew it," Augustin said.

Andri swallowed. "I have to go."

"Do you need me to come with you?" Trevor asked.

"You can do that?"

"It isn't recommended, but yes," Augustin answered for Trevor.

"No, I think I'll be just fine."

"I'll be watching in the pool. If you get in trouble, I'll come."

Trevor and Augustin followed Andri down the hallway into the seer pool room.

"Good luck," they said.

Without hesitating, Andri stepped into the pool.

"What are you doing here? You should be at the edge with the others." A woman pushed at him until he was standing next to the crater of an active volcano. Molten lava bubbled far below him. The smell of sulfur burned his nostrils. He was dressed the same as the other boys around him. White shirt, black pants, with a red belt tied around his waist.

A large man in a black robe read from a scroll. "I, the priest of Avendore, have talked to the red god. The red god has declared it wants one of you this year also. The boy he has selected to appease his anger is Jules. Come forward, Jules."

The boy next to Andri stepped over to the priest, visibly shaking.

"You, Jules, will save our people from the anger of the red god by your sacrifice. Step up on the ramp. If you jump quickly, you won't have to dwell on it. Go on."

Jules stepped up on a stone outcropping, poised to jump into the volcano.

"There is no red god. He's lying. Don't waste your life." Andri jumped and pulled Jules away from the abyss. Dragging Jules behind him, Andri fled into the jungle. The terrain steepened and soon the two of them went rolling down an embankment.

Trees broke their decent and they rested against one, breathing hard.

"Find them! We must kill the infidel." Andri heard the priest bellowing, along with footfalls of men running through the dense jungle, as they tried to locate the boys.

"What are you doing? I was just about to save my people from the red god." Jules brushed the dirt from his clothes. His shirt was stained by the red soil of the area. "Now see what you've done."

"It's molten rock. The volcano has no feeling and cannot talk to priests or anyone else. It's all a lie. The priest, he's lying, and you were going to die for nothing."

"Over here!" Jules waved his hands over his head at a group of men searching for them.

Soon the two of them were surrounded. Andri was seized by three of the larger men and pulled up off the ground. All of them made their way back up to the rim of the volcano.

"Ah, if it isn't the infidel. You have angered the red god. You must die," the priest decreed.

"What did the red god say? If he's angry, why hasn't anything changed? He sits there as before, bubbling and steaming. Wouldn't his rage raise the level of lava, or cause the bubbles to come more rapidly?"

"Shut up that child," the priest ordered.

A man clapped his hand over Andri's mouth.

"Now, Jules, your destiny awaits. Step up upon the ramp."

Jules smiled as he stepped up.

Andri dug his foot into the foot of the man holding his mouth. The man let out a yelp and released his hand.

"Don't die for nothing, Jules!"

With a leap, Jules jumped over the edge. His body barely made a splash as it entered the lava.

"Nooo!" Andri howled.

"I said, shut up that child," snapped the priest. "Throw him into the volcano."

Two men moved Adri towards the edge.

"Wait," another man walked out from the midst of the crowd. "You do not represent the law of this land."

"He has angered the red god. He must die."

"We have never had an unwilling sacrifice to the red god. It is not your place to determine whether the boy lives or dies."

"But the red god has declared it."

Many in the crowd murmured. The man raised his hand. "I am the advisor to the chancellor. It is he who will determine the fate of this boy."

"But…" the priest stomped his foot. "You are angering the red god."

The advisor walked up to the rim. "How do you know that? The boy is right; the red god's demeanor has not changed."

"Sacrilege," the priest hissed.

"What say the people?" the advisor asked. "Should we throw the boy in even though there has never been an unwilling sacrifice to the red god?"

Nos and yesses filled the air.

"We will let the chancellor decide this."

Chapter Ten

Many tents dotted the base of the volcano. They took Andri into the largest one. There, lying surrounded by pillow and blankets sat the largest man Andri had ever seen, not tall, but round. A bowl of cherries and grapes sat in front of the man. He ate another as Andri was pushed into the tent.

"Chancellor, we have brought before you this child who interrupted our ceremony." The advisor brought Andri forward.

"Is the deed done? Has the red god been appeased?"

"Yes, your majesty." The priest stepped forward. "We were able to carry on with our ceremony despite the interruption, but the red god is angry. We need to throw this boy into the volcano."

The chancellor stopped eating and looked up. "An unwilling sacrifice? I've never heard of such a thing."

"The red god demands it."

"How is it, when I was a boy, that the red god only wanted a sacrifice every five years? Now, after you became the priest, it is a yearly event. We'll run out of boys before too long."

"The red god grows restless."

"Sire," the advisor interrupted. "We have never had an unwilling sacrifice."

"It is as I said, the boy must die. He cannot interrupt our rites and ceremonies, but he will not be thrown into the volcano."

"But…" the priest began.

"Depart," the chancellor ordered.

Everyone filed out except for the advisor, Andri, and the two men holding him.

"What do you have to say for yourself?" the chancellor asked. He took another mouthful.

"The priest is lying. You cannot talk to rocks. The volcano is only a mountain with molten rock in it. It doesn't matter how many children you throw in it, it will erupt when it will erupt, and nothing can, or will change that."

He stopped eating again. "A very interesting point of view." Turning to his advisor, the chancellor asked, "What do you make of all this?"

"If he were a true priest, he would have known that you never sacrifice those who are unwilling. I don't think he speaks for the red god."

"No, I suppose not. We will find another priest, one that does not bring us up to this godforsaken place every year. One that actually speaks for the red god."

"There is no red god," Andri protested.

"Of course, there is, didn't you stand there and look down into his mouth?" the advisor asked.

The chancellor pointed at the door of the tent. "Take the boy away, we will remove his head in the morning. Meanwhile, bring me my supper."

Andri spent hours tied to a pole outside the chancellor's tent. He looked up as two men approached. "Augustin, Trevor." He whispered loudly.

"Shh." Trevor put his finger up to his lips. He stood guard as Augustin cut the ropes. "Let's get out of here."

They had only walked behind the tent, before they found themselves climbing out of the seer pool.

When they stepped onto dry ground, Andri hugged both. "Thank you for saving me."

"Did you think we were going to let them chop off your head?" Augustin asked.

"It would have made a terrible mess," Trevor added.

Andri sat down on the ground, dejectedly. "I failed in my mission."

Aladar's face appeared in the seer pool. "You did not fail, Andri. Jules' fate was sealed before you arrived. You could not change that. The chancellor will die soon of a heart attack and the advisor will take over. He will overthrow the priest and not name another one in his stead. He will go up to the volcano often to look into the mouth of the red god. Your words will echo in his mind. When you said, 'You cannot talk to rocks,' his heart was touched."

"Come, Andri, we will celebrate by eating a Torkas egg," Augustin said. "I'm sure Trevor will be willing to share since he doesn't like them anyway."

"Wait, you knew I don't like them?"

"Yes, and every time I bring you one, I watch the grimace on your face as you force it down. It's been great fun."

"I can't believe you would do that to me."

It felt good to Andri to be able to laugh.

That night at dinner, the three of them sat around talking. Trevor stretched out his long legs, while Augustin pushed his food around with his fork. "I'm tired of this food. I want some Kartollian Boar, slow-roasted over the flames of a bonfire."

"Go get some, then," Trevor said.

"I think I will." Augustin stood up and walked towards the seer pool room.

"Wait, you can come and go as you please?" Andri asked. "I thought we were stuck here,"

"No, we have the whole universe at our fingertips. That's why there aren't many travelers in the cafeteria at any one time. We wouldn't all fit in this room anyway. We all fit in the great hall, up above the seer pool. We don't use that often, though, only for ceremonies."

"How do you go from place to place?"

"Just think of a time and place you want to be while you walk into the seer pool. You need to know more about the planets around you, though. You don't want to go to somewhere in the middle of a Galderian invasion."

"Wow, really?"

"Yes, but you must be available to go on missions at the drop of a hat. You had better stick to exploring this planet before you venture too far out into the universe."

"How do I do that?" Andri asked eagerly.

"Walk past the seer pool and up to the corridor you came through when you first came down here. If you go left, you will end up at the temple. If you turn right, you will end up in town. You'll have to use your palm print to get out and back in, so keep track of where you left from."

"I would love to try that." Andri's grin gave away his excitement.

Soon Augustin came back in the room, carrying a big box. "You have to try this, Andri." He sat it on the table. "Kartollian Boar, the best tasting meat in the galaxy."

"Did you get any sauces?" Trevor asked, as he grabbed three plates off the counter.

"Of course. I got the Herdrea sauce you love so much."

Andri peeked into the box. A hind quarter of a large animal steamed on a platter, surrounded by bottles of different colored liquids.

"Pass the blue sauce." Trevor stood at Andri's shoulder.

Andri grabbed the bottle for him and watched as Trevor poured it over his meat.

"Better stick to the green sauce on your first try." Augustin handed Andri a plate full of meat and the bottle.

"Thanks." He sat down to eat. The meat melted in his mouth. He barely had to chew it at all.

Trevor's face went beet red and drops of sweat appeared on his forehead. He fanned himself with his free hand between bites. "This is so good. It's so good."

Chapter Eleven

There was no way of telling night from day in the world under the stone. Trevor had explained it simply, "Sleep when you're tired."

Andri wanted to see the surface, to see the sun again. He walked into the cafeteria.

A grey-haired Dorik, one of the original travelers, came up to him. "You came between meals, but I'm in a good mood. What can I cook for you?"

"Just a glass of milk?"

Dorik laughed. "Your companions would be asking for a bottle of beer right about now. A glass of milk. I can do that. In fact, I'll join you."

Soon, Dorik came back with two glasses of milk. He sat across from Andri.

"Can I ask you a question?"

"You just did." Dorik smiled.

"Why don't you go on missions anymore?"

Dorik took a deep breath, meeting Andri's eyes. "I've seen so much death and misery. I'll let the less experienced travelers take their turn. Midrel feels the same way. We've done our share. We're happy cooking, cleaning, and gathering supplies from across the galaxy."

"Do you get up to the surface ever?"

"Yes, I love taking a stroll in the park right next to the exit. There is a beach not far from there also. The water is fresh, not salty, so I do splash around in it."

"I want to see that," Andri said.

"Go up to the upper level and turn right. Follow that corridor to the end. Your hand acts as a key. Find the smooth part of the stone and put your hand there on the pad against the wall. The park is just to your left and the beach is to the right and down about five blocks. Check the sky first thing. If there are three suns, then it's too hot to be up on the surface. If there are only one or two, you're safe."

Andri jumped up. "I'm going."

"Take your card with you," Dorik called after him.

Stopping in his tracks, Andri asked. "What card?"

"Your money card. It's in the top drawer of your desk."

"How do I have a money card?"

"You do have a lot to learn. Planets and governments reward us for our work. The travelers are allowed to use currency cards. Just don't go crazy. We have everything we need down here, but a treat once in a while is allowed."

"Money card, thanks." Andri ran off.

When the stone door opened at the end of the long hall, sunshine flowed in. Andri squinted. *Two suns!* He walked out onto the street. Looking left, he watched young children playing in the park. *Too noisy.* He turned right.

He passed by beautiful houses, much larger than the mud hut he lived in. They were two stories high, with balconies and railings. Curtains at each window rustled in the light breeze. Soon he was standing on sand. Taking off his shoes, he walked towards the water. He reached the edge and stopped. The sounds of the waves splashing against the sand enthralled him as he gazed out upon it.

"Don't just stand there. I need help with my battlements."

Andri had been so intent on the water, he didn't even see the girl at his feet building a sandcastle.

"Hold the wall so I can pack sand on the bottom to keep it from falling down," the blonde girl in pigtails and a pink swimsuit asked again.

Andri dropped to his knees and held the wall for her as she supported it with sand.

"There, you can let go now."

Andri sat down and wiped the sand off his hands. "It's really detailed. You did a good job."

"Thank you. It's my best yet. My brother builds them better, though, with towers and keeps. One time he even built a drawbridge out of some sticks and twine."

"I'm Andri."

She shook his hand. "Lilly."

"Good to meet you. Lilly, do you live around here?"

"No, we have to take the hover bus to get here. You?"

He nodded. "Close, but I'm new here."

"How old are you? I mean in standard years, not in Gad years. Other planets have night and day, not like here. Did you come from another planet? Did it have nighttime?"

"I'm sixteen in standard years. I have no idea how old I am in Gad years. I do come from a planet that has days and nights. Nighttime is cooler, and the stars come out and dot the sky above. It's a beautiful thing."

"I've never seen a star. I'm fourteen in standard years. In Gad years, I'm only three."

"So, I would be four in Gad years?"

"Something like that."

A woman had come up and stood over them. "Beautiful job, Lilly, and you met a friend." Andri looked up and the woman gasped. "Andri!" She bowed, it's a pleasure to meet you, Time God."

Lilly turned to him, "You're a Time God?"

"I'm afraid so, but how does your mother know that?"

"We all watched the broadcast of the trials when you were selected. Everyone was rooting for you. We all held our breath when Buliston tried to stab you, and then when you entered the stone, we all clapped."

"Thank you. I didn't know anyone was watching me."

"Yes, of course, but that was years ago. Lilly was too young to remember back then."

Years ago?

Andri stood up. "I should go."

"Mom, we should invite him to lunch." Lily insisted. "He can see how people on this planet live."

"We would love it if you came to lunch, Time God," the mother replied.

"Yes, thank you. I would be honored."

The hover bus system didn't seem that difficult to Andri. He memorized the route, just in case he wanted to see Lily again. *She's only fourteen. What are you doing?* Shaking himself out of his thoughts, he exited the bus in front of one of the two-story houses he had seen all over town.

The mother unlocked the door. As he entered, Andri could see all the pictures of the travelers on her wall, his included. A few he didn't recognize; he would ask about them when he returned to the seer pool. The mother cooked a wonderful meal of stuffed fowl. It reminded him of turkeys from his own planet, but they were much smaller.

Lilly pointed to the back yard. "The swimming pool is almost done. You should come back soon to swim in it."

"Yes I would like that."

After the meal, Andri bid them goodbye. He managed to get on the right bus to get to the stone door. It opened at the touch of his palm and he walked back down to his room.

Later, at dinner, Trevor and Augustin sat across from him. The two chatted as they ate. Soon Augustin said, "What's wrong with you today, Andri? You haven't said a word and you're not eating."

"I've already eaten and I was just thinking."

"He went up to the surface," Trevor said. "What did you find?"

"Well, I met someone."

Augustin shook his head. "Let me put an end to that right now. Relationships don't work. You're a traveler. Time has no meaning to you."

"She's too young anyway. I wasn't thinking of romance. I was thinking of her as a friend."

Trevor shrugged. "That doesn't work either."

"Why not?" Andri asked.

"Because," Trevor answered, 'Time changes them. They get old and die and you lose them, over and over again. It's better to protect your heart."

"Then why are there no female Time Gods then?" Andri asked.

"There are. Aladar is one of us, but she never travels. She's the one who figures out where to send us," Trevor said. "She is also the one who picks the travelers, and she doesn't like other women around."

"Really? I thought it was Estran who was in charge of the Time Gods."

"Estran talks to Aladar. She lives in real-time, but is a Time God, so she never ages. Estran will grow old and she'll replace him with someone else," Trevor explained.

"This is all very confusing."

Augustin nodded, "That's why you're only an apprentice. When you understand it, you'll be a full-fledge traveler."

Chapter Twelve

"Andri."

The sound of Aladar's voice woke him from a deep sleep. He stood up and dressed. Walking down the corridor without a word, he stepped into the seer pool.

A blast from an energy weapon hit the rocks above his head. Instinctively, he ducked. Several more blasts hit the area around him.

"Die, you Tescire scum!" A young man leaped up from behind the rocks, blasted away at the unseen enemy.

Energy blasts zinged all around, barely missing him. Andri rushed toward him, grabbing him and pulling him down, just in the nick of time. More energy blasts hit right where he was standing.

"What are you doing? We're the Caldor Youth Corps. We have to kill as many Tescire as possible."

Andria scanned the area. A group of children cowered behind rocks behind them. "Our job is to get them to safety, not get ourselves killed."

The boy looked at the children and nodded. "There is a cave down there where we can hide them."

"Let's go." Andri motion to the children, and they followed them.

Enemy fire slackened as they crept along the cliffside.

"Where's your gun?"

Andri looked for a weapon, but he didn't have one. "I don't know. I must have dropped it."

The young man shook his head but led on. When they came upon the bodies of several soldiers, he picked up a gun and handed it to Andri. "Don't lose this one."

A few minutes later, they reached the cave entrance. A young girl came up, her brown hair in pigtails, and threw her arms around the young man's neck. "Radic, I'm scared."

"Lead the others into the cave, Emilia. I'll be standing guard out here."

She took a deep breath, wiped her tears, and nodded. Motioning, the others followed her.

Andri took up position next to Radic.

"I've never seen you at the meetings. Who are you?" Radic asked.

"Andri. I'm new."

"You picked a bad time to join, right before the Tescire invasion."

Andri swallowed. "Yes. What are our chances of winning?"

"Reports say this area is their main thrust. They are not gaining ground anywhere else. In the Teerick Sector, they are even being pushed back. It's only a matter of time till we rid our planet of the swine."

Andri nodded. "Good." He saw movement off to the left. "They've followed us."

Radic crouched down and took aim.

Andri touched his shoulder. "No heroics. We have to protect the children."

Energy hits flashed a white streak in the air, striking the cliff face behind Andri and Radic. They returned fire.

The intensity of the enemy fire increased. "Back into the cave," Radic ordered. The two of them kept firing as they retreated.

Choosing a group of rocks to hide behind, they took up a position inside the cave.

Three enemy soldiers entered the cave but were quickly cut down.

"Duck," Radic yelled as two metal spheres were thrown into the cave. An ear-splitting explosion and a flash of brilliant white shook the cave. Dirt trickled down from the ceiling. Seven enemies rushed in. Andri shook the ringing out of his ears and fired at the figures. A moment later, Radic's gun came to life. The duel between the two groups lasted several minutes. It finally slackened. The last of the enemy rushed back out of the cave entrance. The others lay dead in front of Andri.

"We did it." Andri lifted up his weapon in victory, but when he looked over, Radic, lay motionless on the ground. An energy blast burn blackening his left side. Andri crawled over to Radic, touching him, he knew he was dead.

"Radic!" the little girl had sneaked forward. She wrapped her arms around Radic's neck. "Brother, don't leave me."

"We can't do anything for him. Get back down the cave," Andri hissed.

"No," she picked up Radic's gun. "I'll fight."

"I'll keep you safe. Get back down the cave and help the others."

"I'll help them by helping you."

Andri didn't have time to argue further. He saw movement at the cave's entrance. Andri raised his weapon and took aim. The girl pushed it back down. "They're our soldiers. Don't shoot."

Andri leaned back against the rocks and released the breath he didn't know he was holding. A scruffy man with stripes on his arm examined the dead, then walked up to Andri. "There were only two of you?"

Andri nodded.

"Well done. We'll take it from here."

"There's a group of children further down the cave," Andri said.

The soldier motioned his men forward.

Not long afterwards, at the cave entrance, a transport craft set down. Andri and the children boarded it. They were flown to an evacuation center.

When Andri exited the craft, an officer spoke into his communicator, then pointed it at Andri's face. "Is this him?"

"Yes," responded a voice.

"Follow me," the officer ordered.

Andri trudged along behind him. They entered a building with many wounded soldiers sitting or lying on the floor.

An officer with a lot of ribbons on his chest handed out medals. When he turned, he smiled. "This is the Youth Corp member? You have been brave today." He pinned a metal to Andri's chest.

"Radic was the brave one. I just followed his lead."

The officer replied, "He will be awarded posthumously."

Andri couldn't stand being in the stuffy building any longer. He excused himself and walked out the back door.

Finding himself in the seer pool, he walked up the steps. "Aladar, I failed again. Radic died."

"I did not send you there to rescue Radic. In fact, the person I sent you there to rescue has searched for you for many years. I'm going to grant her wish and send you back. Reenter the pool."

Andri turned on his heels and went back down into the seer pool.

Music softly hummed in the background. All around Andri were adults drinking and talking. One lady, in a purple dress with a tiara adorning her brown hair, walked around the room greeting the guests. The guests were wearing uniforms, suits, or ball gowns.

Andri was back in the uniform he had worn during the battle. The sweat stains, blood splatters, and dirt had all been washed out. With a neatly pressed and supporting the medal he had been given, Andri felt like a stuffed shirt.

He faded into the back of the room, away from the hubbub.

The lady, however made her way to that side of the room. She paused in front of him. "A little young to be here, aren't you?"

"I wasn't too young to fight."

Her eyes softened. "My brother was your age when he died fighting for the planet. In fact, you look so much like the young man who fought beside him. He might have been a relative of yours. Do you know a man named Andri?"

"I *am* Andri." Aladar's words echoed in his mind. He was granting her wish as Aladar requested.

She gasped, "Are you named after your father? I've been looking for him for years."

"No, I am Andri. I was there when your brother, Radic was killed. I am a Time God. I do not age."

Her eyes went round. "You're Andri? Thank you for being there. Thank you for saving my life!" She wrapped his arms around him and held him tight.

Many of the guests gathered around her to see what was happening. One of her bodyguards came up to her. "Is everything all right, Prime Minister Emilia?"

"Everyone, come here." She held up her hand to get their attention. "This is the boy that saved my life during the invasion. It is he who risked his. For all of you who do not believe in the Time Gods, here is one standing before you. They sent a Time God to help our planet."

Andri grew restless as the crowd gathered close, chattering. He'd never been asked so many questions. Two or three at a time, in fact. He did his best to field them.

Emilia took pity on him eventually. "That's it for now. We need to let Andri rest." Pulling him aside, she gave him one last thank you before letting him go on his way.

Coming out of the seer pool Andri stopped. "Thank you for letting me see what happened. You were right in sending me back. I didn't fail."

"No, you didn't. Now, go and get some rest. Other missions await," Aladar replied.

Chapter Thirteen

It was a new day and Andri headed up to the surface to see Lilly. He checked at the beach, but she wasn't there. Hoping he hadn't missed her, he took the hover bus to her house. His heart thundering as he walked up. He didn't know why he was so nervous. He knocked on the door.

Her mother answered, "Hello. Andri, I haven't seen you in a while."

"Oh?" *I was here only yesterday.* "Is Lilly here?"

"She's on a date, but should be home soon."

"A date? She's fourteen." It blurted out, he felt both jealousy and astonishment.

Her mother laughed. "You Time Gods lose track, don't you? She's sixteen."

Sixteen! He managed to not say it out loud this time. The door behind him opened and Lilly and a boy stepped in.

"Andri!" She ran over and hugged him. "I haven't seen you in a year. You used to come over a lot, but then you stopped. What's going on?"

"I've been, um, busy," he stammered. She was as tall as he now. Her pigtails were gone, replaced with long hair that curled at the ends.

"It's so good to see you. Andri, this is Danis." She flushed as she introduced him. Andri could tell she was nervous.

"I just wanted to say hi but didn't want to take your whole evening. I have to go."

Lily seemed relieved but protested his early departure anyway. Her mother smiled that knowing smile

Andri had seen his own mother do. He retreated out the door.

Sixteen! His mind couldn't wrap itself around that concept. Hadn't he been at the beach with her yesterday?

He arrived back at his apartment. He threw himself on his bed, utterly drained. Not wanting to talk to anyone, he turned off the lights.

"All Time Gods to the seer pool."

"Lights," Andri said. He slipped on some sweatpants and a t-shirt. It didn't matter what he wore, he would be wearing something different when he arrived at wherever he was headed. He walked into the room to find the other travelers donning helmets, checking energy weapons, and putting on body armor.

"What's going on?" Andri asked.

"Time Bandits. They have Eldoren. We have to go rescue him," Trevor said.

"What are time bandits and who is Eldoren?"

"You've never met Eldoran because he doesn't have a room near the seer pool. He does long-term assignments and is gone for years at a time. The time bandits are those trying to take over time and interplanetary travel so they can control the galaxy. Our job is to stop them."

Andri took the white fire suit off the cart. It fit perfectly. Then he grabbed the black body armor and wrapped it around his chest. Donning the helmet, he picked up an energy weapon and the round cylinder with a pullcord out the back. "What is this?"

"Whoa, don't point that at me." Trevor pushed the end of it aside. "Take the strap, clip it, then sling it over your shoulder. We'll worry about that later."

"Okay."

Andri scanned the room. Even Dorik and Midrel were there, preparing with the rest. Dorik motioned with his head. "It's time. We all need to be in the pool at the same time or we will arrive staggered." He turned to Andri. "Aladar is putting us there in a time and place that there are only bad guys in the building. If it moves, shoot it. Do you understand?"

Andri nodded and moved toward the pool.

When they were all neck deep, Dorik gave the signal. "Now."

They stood shoulder to shoulder in a warehouse building, surrounded a chair in the middle of the room which had a man tied to it. As if on cue, they all started shooting. For some reason, all the time bandits were looking out doors and windows, as they were expecting an attack from the outside.

Andri shot a man standing near the middle window. A woman came from a door down the hall. Andri paused, hoping she had just been caught in the middle, but then she raised a weapon. Before Andri could shoot, Trevor took her out.

"Shoot everyone," he hissed.

Andri scanned the room, but all the time bandits were dead on the floor. The travelers walked up to the walls. Trevor motioned for Andri to follow him. He pulled the cylindrical object from his back. "Hold it like this and then pull the cord." Trevor pointed his at the wall and pulled the string. Fire came out the end.

Andri followed suit, setting fire to the nearest wall. When the building was engulfed in flames, the travelers stood back into the center of the room. Dorkin had cut the man on the chair loose. Andri assumed it was Eldoren.

"Now would be a good time to get us out of here Aladar."

Andri waited his turn to climb out of the seer pool. He watched as Eldoren, supported by two other travelers, was dragged out of the pool. They took him down the hall to the infirmary. Augustin would take care of him. He was the only one to have studied medicine before he became a traveler.

Everyone hung up their body armor and helmets on hooks. Dorik and Midrel took all the clothes away in a cart.

"Good job today, Andri," Augustin put his hand on Andri's shoulder.

"I froze when I saw the woman. She couldn't have been over twenty. Trevor had to shoot her."

"They're all dead, we are all alive, and you didn't have to kill the woman. It ended well."

"Will I have to worry about time bandits capturing me?"

"No, the missions we do are in and out. They won't have time to track us down. It's the likes of Eldoren they were able to find because he was on a long-term assignment. That is a rare mission."

Andri stopped in front of his door.

"What are you doing?" Augustin asked.

"Going to my quarters."

"No, we're going to celebrate getting Eldoren back alive."

"I don't feel much like celebrating. I just killed a man," Andri replied.

"All the more reason not to be alone, come on."

"Shouldn't you be checking on Eldoren?"

"What he needs is rest and he's getting that. Come on."

Andri shrugged but followed.

When they arrived at the cafeteria, a feast greeted them. The center of the tables was heaped with food of every kind. Cured meats and cooked meats with all sorts of side dishes.

"Here, try this," Trevor handed Andri a plate full of what looked like chicken legs. "Santorian Gullen Fowl."

Andri took a bite. "It's so good. Like a rich dark meat."

Trevor piled more food on Andri's plate.

"Wait, I thought you were angry at me for not killing the woman."

Trevor shrugged. "You didn't expect to see her. It won't happen again."

"No, it won't."

An hour later, the only ones left in the cafeteria were Trevor, Augustin, Andri, and Dorik.

Andri rubbed his overfull stomach. "Oh, I ate too much."

Dorik put the last of the leftovers into the kitchen, "That's it, I'm going to sleep this off."

"Lilly is sixteen. How is that possible? I just saw her yesterday." Andri blurted out to no one in particular.

Dorik stopped in his tracks. "You didn't tell him how to move around in time?"

"He's in a relationship. we didn't want him to get hurt," Trevor answered.

"Don't listen to them," Dorik replied. "You can visit anywhere at any time. Go to the seer pool and concentrate on where you want to be, and when. It will take you there. When you want to come back, call Aladar, and she'll bring you back."

That's all there is to it?" Andri asked.

"I hate to be a bearer of bad news, but relationships don't work," Trevor replied.

"Let him find out for himself," Dorik said. "Besides, young love, it's so cute."

Andri calmly left the room. Once the door closed, he ran to the end of the corridor. Standing in front of the seer pool, he concentrated. He would arrive the very next day he met Lilly. He stepped in.

He found himself on the beach again. Lilly was building another sandcastle while her mother read a book in a beach chair. He watched Lilly from a distance, not wanting to disturb the scene. Before he got his courage up to walk over to her, the mother said, "Hi, Andri."

Lilly looked up. "Andri, come over here." She motioned him over. "I'm building a bigger one this time. Here, hold the base of the tower and I'll connect a wall to it."

He did it. He didn't tell her he wasn't good at it, but as he watched her, he became better and better.

Soon he had a proper tower. She attached her wall. "There," she said with a smile. "It's done."

"What will you do with it now?"

"By tomorrow, the inland sea will swallow it up as the tide comes in."

"But all that work," he protested.

She smiled and patted his knee. "We will be another one, bigger and better. I'll be back here in three days. Can you meet me?"

"I'll try."

They talked another hour while the waves drew closer to the sandcastle.

"Come, Lilly." Her mother rose. "We need to get inside. Two more suns will rise before these two set. It will be too hot to stay here."

Lilly turned to him, "Will you come with us?"

"No, I'd better get back."

"Come on, we have an indoor pool now. This planet is too hot to be without it."

"I don't have a swimsuit," he said.

"We'll stop and get you one on the way home," the mother interjected.

"Okay, sounds fun."

Hours later, when he'd been in the pool, played games, and told stories, he realized it was late, so he headed home.

"Bye, Andri," she hugged him as he left.

He walked out the front door, heaving a sigh and then said, "Aladar, I'm ready to go back." Walking out of the seer pool, he made his way down the hall to the cafeteria. He wanted to see if his friends were still there. The room was dark, so he went to his quarters. Pulling a book off the shelf, he read up on the history of his assigned planet. Many books sat on the shelf, but he had an eternity to read them.

Chapter Fourteen

Andri sat looking over the rushing waters of a river. The area was beautiful. The valley walls were steep and full of evergreen trees. A brick pathway ran next to the river's edge. Scanning the area, he saw no obvious signs of danger. *Why am I here?*

His clothes were a rough weave with patches, much like the clothes he had grown up wearing. He watched the river flow by, not noticing that someone had come up behind him.

"We don't bow to our prince now?"

Andri turned and bowed. "Sorry, my prince, I didn't see you."

"Pay better attention in the future, serf." The Prince folded his arms. "What is your name?"

"Andri."

"Andri what?"

He shrugged, "Just Andri."

"What is your family name?"

"I don't have one."

"Everyone has a family name. Whose servant are you?"

"I'm no one's servant."

The prince took a step back. To Andri he looked like he'd just been slapped. The prince stared for a moment before saying, "You're my servant, then. I claim you."

"Why do I have to be someone's servant?" Andri's asked.

"It's the way of things."

"Whose servant are you?"

"Why, such insolence. I'm royalty, I'm not a servant. Come, let's get you to the castle. The queen is in an impossible mood today, so we'll avoid her."

The prince turned and walked back up the path he'd come from. Is this a dream or a mission? Andri wasn't sure. It didn't really matter anyway. He would get back to his room and friends after he woke, or the mission was over. *I wonder where Lilly is.* His heart sank. She could be an old woman by now as far as he knew. Trevor was right, relationships were hard.

Soon a large wall with a gate made out of timbers and iron appeared around a corner. The stone walkway led right up to it.

"It's the prince, open the gate," a watchman called out.

Chains engaged the pulleys, clanking. Slowly, the gate opened. The prince strode in like he was walking along a parade ground. A smaller trail led through the house-lined street and up to the palace sitting upon the hill.

Andri had seen many fine and exquisite palaces in his time, but this wasn't one of them. It was made of brownstone and barely two stories tall. It didn't have the towers and turrets he expected, not even archer slots in the walls. The prince opened the door and walked in. Andri hesitated.

"Come in," the prince motioned.

Andri scanned the room. Except for a narrow ornate rug, the room was plain. The walls were the same brown rock as the exterior. Torches in the corner lit it as there were only two thin windows. A hall led straight ahead. Two doors were on either side.

Not two feet from the entrance stood a tired-looking old woman with a tiara. She frowned at the prince "Where have you been? The king has been asking about you. No one could find you in the city."

"I took a walk down by the river."

"Who's this street urchin you have with you? How dare you bring him into the palace?" She glared at Andri.

"He's my servant."

"What? I've not assigned a servant to you."

"He was down by the river and was no one's servant so I made him mine."

She turned to Andri, "What is your family name? And don't lie to me."

"I have no family name. I am no one's servant."

"Impossible, you are lying. He must be a spy."

"I am no spy. If you wish me to depart, I am willing."

"He stays," the prince folded his arms.

"Humph," the queen retorted. "At least get him some clothes befitting a servant to a prince. Your father still wants you."

"Come with me," the prince said to Andri.

They entered a room to the side of the main hall. It was just as plain, except for a bed in the center where an aged man lay, being attended to by two others. The two men stepped back when the prince approached.

"Father, how are you?" the prince asked.

"The healers say it won't be long now."

The prince looked into the face of the healer as if to confirm what he heard. The healer nodded. "You must go on. The country depends on you. There will be chaos without you."

"No, I must die, it's the only way I can get away from that woman. I should have listened to you, son, when you said not to marry her. She's trouble. At least marrying her stopped a war, except the ones I've been fighting with her for the past five years." He looked up. "Who is that with you?"

"This is my servant."

"She's finally let you have a servant? I thought that would never happen."

"It wasn't her, I found him by the river. He didn't have a family name, so I took him for my own."

"Good for you. I told her you needed a servant of your own. She wouldn't listen."

The king started a coughing spell. The two healers closed in. One motioned the price to leave.

Waiting until he reached his own room, the prince collapsed on the bed in a sobbing heap. Andri stood there not knowing what to do. *Should I have not followed him? Should I leave?* He stepped back quietly, intent on exiting.

The prince composed himself. "Can you bring me a wet washcloth?"

Andri looked around, trying to find one in the room.

"From the kitchen."

"Oh, um, where's the kitchen?"

"At the end of the long hallway."

Andri bowed, leaving the door into the main foyer, then walked to the end of the hall. The kitchen was a beehive of activity. One cook sprinkled flour on rolls before she rolled them out, another plucked a goose. Two more stood over pots and stirred.

"What are you doing in my kitchen. Get out!" A large woman with a stained apron and a chef's hat stood over him.

"The prince wants a wet washcloth."

"Who are you?" she asked.

"I'm the prince's servant. I'm Andri."

The woman smiled. "It's about time he got his own servant. That queen has been treating him as a servant." She grabbed a cloth out of a drawer and poured water from a pitcher on to it. "Here you go."

"Thank you." He gave her a slight bow then headed back out the door.

Andri overheard her saying as he left, "I'm going to like that one. He has manners."

Arriving back, Andri handed it to the prince who wiped his face with it. "No sense in letting the queen know I've been crying. She'll take it for a weakness."

Chapter Fifteen

The prince and Andri sat down by the river listening to the endless flow of water. Andri hated the outfit the queen had made for him. He gazed down at the yellow sleeves, the bright white wide collar digging into his neck. He looked and felt ridiculous. He would rather be wearing the raggedy clothes. He grew up wearing raggedy clothes. He was used to them.

"When my mother was alive, I used to come down here to watch the water. There were six knights to protect me. Since the new queen has taken over, I'm on my own." The prince stared straight ahead.

The prince seemed deep in thought, but Andri said anyway, "Tell me about this queen you have. You do not seem to be on good terms with her."

The prince looked up. "You are supposed to address me as Sire. That was one of the things the queen is mad about today, you weren't supposed to look her in the eyes when you talked to her and you didn't call her Madame."

"Do you want me to address you as Sire, then?"

The prince smiled, "Not while we're alone. I love it that you made the queen mad though. Not that it is a difficult task. There was a war when I was young. The land of Middourin was slowly taking over our kingdom. My father married the princess of that land to end the war and regain his kingdom. Now, that he's dying, they are building up their army again. The queen stops us from doing the same. They have eight hundred loyal knights who have allied themselves with the land of Middourin. We have five hundred. It is a matter of time until we lose."

"What will happen then?"

"The queen takes over our land and I get my head chopped off," the prince swallowed involuntarily.

"What?" Andri gasped.

"It's the way of things."

"You can't get more soldiers?"

"No, the knights are of royal blood. They have the breeding to be fighting men. Their horses are powerful, and their swords sharp. We need to talk them into coming to our side, but the queen prevents me from doing that, and my father is too sickly to do it himself."

"You don't need an entire army of only knights. You can have pikemen and archers too. They don't have to be royals, either. Release men from servitude and allow them to be in the army."

The prince stared at him wide-eyed. "You can't be serious. Do you even know a thing about war? That is not the way things are done."

Andri leaned back against a tree. "Even at my age, I have seen war. I have been in wars. I have killed men. No one wins in a war. You only have those who lose less."

"You've seen war? You are not a royal. You are not from around here. Do they do it differently in other lands?" the prince asked.

"Yes, much differently. The royals lead vast armies of men at arms. You have men with swords and shields, archers, pikemen, and knights. They all work in unison. A horse will not charge a wall of men with pikes. When their horses stop in front, the archers send volleys into them, then the knights go on the attack."

The prince stood up and began pacing back and forth. "Where do I get the men?"

"Not everyone needs to be someone's servant. Release them from servitude and pay them for being part of the army."

He resumed his pacing. Then he finally stopped. "I'm going to do it, and you will show me how. The first person I set free from servitude is you."

"Thank you, Sire."

The rest of the day they talked about how to organize this army and Andri drew pictures of the different weapons. That night, he went to bed, glad to be out of the silly servant's uniform.

He climbed up the steps of the seer pool. "I need to go back. I wasn't done."

"You accomplished your mission. You gave the land the idea of free men. The king died that very night. He named his son as heir. The queen fled the castle and went to her own land. She didn't have the support she had supposed, so the war never happened. Meanwhile, the idea of men living free had come to the land."

"Did the prince raise his army?"

"He did. A mighty army. His land is secure."

Andri hung his head. "Does the prince miss me?"

"He was sad you left, but you can't keep something and set it free at the same time," Aladar replied.

He walked down to the cafeteria. It was dark. Everyone was asleep. Then he remembered Lilly. She would be waiting for him at the beach. *In three days*, she had said. He wanted to see her again. He rushed back down the hall. Entering the seer pool, he was soon standing at the beach. His heart sank when he saw she wasn't there.

He sat dejectedly on the sand. In a few minutes, he played with the sand between his toes.

"Andri, I knew you would come. Mom said you would be out saving worlds from utter destruction, but I knew you would be here." She threw her arms around him in a giant hug.

It felt so good. Not like the hugs his mother used to give him, but it tingled all the way down to his toes.

"Here, I saw a picture of a giant castle on a planet far away. I would love to visit it someday." She handed him a datapad. "This is what we're building. Have you ever been to a castle with kings and queens?"

He nodded, "I just came from there. It was plain and boring, nothing like this."

"Here you start on the outside wall, and I'll begin building the palace. This is going to be amazing."

Hours later, he stumbled back down the hall towards his room.

"Oh, no, you don't. We haven't seen you in days. You're going to come down to the cafeteria and talk to us," Trevor said.

"I'm so tired."

"Yes, I know. You come home from a mission, then go see your girlfriend right away. You're eating away at both ends of the day. I'm going to make sure you're good and tired by this evening, so you go to bed and get some sleep. Come now, breakfast is waiting."

After they ate, Trevor grabbed a box and poured out some dice and picked up two datapads. "It's a game from one of the planets you've been assigned to. These are dice, they have dots on it. You have three rolls to get the numbers you want."

"What's the point of doing that?"

"To get the most points, of course. If you do that, you win."

"What happens then?"

Trevor sighed, "Don't worry about it. You're not going to win anyway. Just shut up and play, will you?"

Chapter Sixteen

He had drifted off to sleep many hours later. "Lights," he said as he woke up. His room was still pitch black. "Lights." Still nothing.

Getting out of bed, he made his way to the door. "Open." No response. He knocked on it and waited. *What did Trevor say about an emergency open panel?* He felt around the door until he located it. Popping it off, a red button illuminated. He pushed it. *Nothing.* Feeling around, he located a dial. Turning it, the door creaked open just wide enough for him to slip out. He only found more darkness. He felt his way down the hall towards the seer pool. The steel door was open.

"Aladar, can you hear me?" He waited a few minutes. Trying to enter the pool, the liquid was cold and brackish. *What's going on? Where is everyone?* His heart raced. "Aladar?"

"Shh, get out of the pool, they will sense you."

"Aladar!" he stepped back.

"Time bandits have attacked the temple. I'm in hiding, I sent all the others away before they cut the power. The seer pool is turned off. I need you to find out what's going on. The palm reader at the end of the corridor is still active. It's on a separate circuit. Don't turn on any lights, but go up to the surface, then report back on what you find."

"Right away." He took two steps, but then turned back. "It's so good to hear your voice." Feeling his way to the palm reader, he put his hand on it. The brightness

blinded him until his eyes adjusted. *Three suns, very bad.*
He stepped out into the sweltering heat.

Smoke rose from the hill where the temple sat.
Once in a while, he could see the flash of energy weapons.
He climbed up the side of the hill. The suns beat down on
his back and sweat poured out in places he didn't know he
could sweat. He neared the crest, he watched as men in the
red robes of the keepers inched closer to the edge of the
temple wall. Three pirates fired at them and the keepers
ducked down.

Andri spied a keeper lying on the ground nearby.
He crawled over to check on him. The man was dead. The
toc'fi lay by his side, but in his hand was an energy pistol.
Andri remembered the pain of the toc'fi hitting him in the
back. This one was set to kill. He picked up the pistol and
repositioned himself. The three pirates were in perfect view
now. He took aim and fired three shots.

The pirates fell dead. Andri felt the point of a toc'fi
against his back. "Who are you?"

When Andri turned, the keeper pulled the toc'fi
away and bowed. "Time God, it is good to see you are all
right."

"Thank you so much for defending us." Andri
bowed also.

"It is our honor."

"Are the grounds secure?"

"They are now. We must get you out of the suns."

"I have to report back." Andri made his way back
down the hill. One of the suns was mercifully setting.
When he opened the door, he stepped in the coolness of the
underground corridor. "Lights." *Still not working.*

He felt his way down towards the seer pool. He shivered from the coolness of his wet clothes. When he arrived back to the room, he called out, "Aladar, the coast is clear."

The lights came on and the pool came to life. One by one, his fellow travelers climbed up out of the seer pool. Trevor was the last one. "Andri, you slept through the whole thing, didn't you? It was a near thing. Time bandits were closing in on the rock itself."

"Yes, sorry I missed it." Andri looked down while he dug the toe of his shoe in the sand around the seer pool.

"At least Aladar sent us somewhere nice. We were at the Inn of the Altar in the Adalian mountains during the feast of summer. They eat for three days without stopping, then the three day fast begins. I'm stuffed. I was so glad we came back right before the fasting started."

"What? You were feasting while people were dying here?"

"It was Aladar's doing. Besides, *you* were sleeping."

They all made their way down to the cafeteria where Dorik poured a hard drink for everyone except Andri. He handed Andri a glass of purple juice.

"I'm ageless. How many generations will I have to survive until I'm treated as an adult around here?" Andri protested.

Dorik picked up another glass, held up the bottle, then looked at Andri. Setting the bottle back down, he said, "I just can't. You look like a kid to me. Drink your juice." He held up his glass. "Here's to surviving another battle with the time bandits, oh and here's to you, Andri. I'm told you were fighting bandits under three suns while we were at the galaxy's biggest party."

They toasted him. Trevor turned to him. "You said you were sleeping."

"No, you said I was sleeping. I just didn't correct you."

After the festivities ended, the others staggered off. Andri raided the food supply. He hadn't been feasting for three days like the other travelers. Sitting down with a sandwich and a salad, he was interrupted by Trevor coming back into the room. "I thought you were in your room. I had to come to say I'm sorry for accusing you of sleeping through the firefight."

Andri shrugged. "It didn't bother me."

"How are you adjusting otherwise?"

Setting down his sandwich Andri said, "Time travel is not what I thought. There are no clear-cut lines between good and evil. When I go on a mission, it's hard to figure out what the right actions are. Several times I thought I was to do one thing, and I feel like a failure when I came back, only to be told by Aladar that what I did was a success."

"That's not the worst of it. I messed up an assignment so badly that she sent Augustin in to fix it."

"Did he?"

"Yes, expertly, but I wasn't given another assignment for three months, our time. Don't worry, if Aladar wants something fixed, she'll get it fixed even if it takes all of us to do it." Trevor stood up and poured himself a drink of water.

"It's hard. One day, I'm consoling a little girl, then the next day I'm shooting bad guys. My time off is spent here. Where's the happiness in all this?"

"Ah, you've reached the point of discouragement. We all get there. Just a minute." He knocked on a couple of doors, and soon Augustin and Dorik joined him. "Our little friend is discouraged. We will give him the pick me up and send him on his way."

"I have just the thing," Dorik said. He grabbed a bottle and a shot glass. He poured the clear liquid in the glass and pushed it over to Andri. "You still look like a kid to me, but you've matured and are a good traveler. Here's your first drink."

Andri eyed the glass for a minute, then brought it slowly to his lips.

"Don't sip it, down the hatch in one gulp," Augustin urged.

Andri obeyed. He coughed twice, turned red, then gasped for air. Holding his hand to his chest, he said, "It burns."

"Of course, it does," Trevor replied. "Dorik only gets the best stuff. Now go to the seer pool, Aladar awaits you."

Chapter Seventeen

Dusk set on the horizon. Andri found himself on the steps of a mansion, next to a bench surrounded by flowers. He looked over the grounds and up at the big stone house but couldn't find a living soul anywhere. He gazed out upon the sunset.

"Andri?"

He turned to see Lilly standing behind him. She rushed up and hugged him.

"Lilly."

Taking a step back, she looked him over. "You haven't aged a bit."

"Time Gods don't age, but you have. How old are you now?"

"I'm fifteen, almost the same age as you. Come sit. I've never seen a sunset before." He held her hand as they sat on the bench. "Are you on some mission to save the planet or something?"

"No, just taking a break. How did you come to be here? Wherever we are, that is."

"This is the planet Anderia. My uncle bade me to come. Gad is in its summer season and most days have three suns, some even have four. You just can't go outside this time of year. They felt sorry for me and brought me here."

They sat there long enough for the sun to go down. She inched closer so he put his arm around her.

"I never realized, but I think I'm afraid of the dark. I've never seen it before."

"You have nothing to fear. I'm here."

The lights in the courtyard came on. Suddenly there were four men with energy weapons pointed at Andri. One talked into his wrist. "The intruder has been found. He has Lilly hostage."

"No," he pulled away from her. "We were only enjoying the sunset."

Another man strode up. "Uncle, this is my friend, Andri. He's visiting me."

The uncle folded his arms. "Andri, eh? How did you get past my security?"

"He's a Time God, he goes when and where he pleases," she replied.

The uncle tilted his head. "What's a Time God doing here?"

"Taking a vacation," Andri replied.

The uncle smiled. "Well, I'll ask the maid to prepare a room for you."

"I don't want to be any trouble. I can stay in the nearest town," Andri replied.

"The nearest town is miles away and rough. I've been beside myself figuring out how to entertain Lilly. My problem is solved with you here." The uncle turned and walked away. The guards disappeared into the darkness.

Andri put his arm around her again, smelling the freshness of her hair. She rested her head on his shoulder. "There are no beaches here. There is a large lake at the base of the chateau, but it has no sand."

"Are you still into building sandcastles? I don't see you much after you turn sixteen."

She sat up. "You've seen me at sixteen?"

"Yes, it will be an awkward moment for you to look forward to. I finished a mission and wanted to see you. I thought it was the very next day after we met, so I went to your house. You were on a date. I was still there when you arrived back home. You seemed happy to see me, but your date wasn't happy at all. I left as soon as possible. I still don't have this time thing down. I did find another way to do it, so I won't embarrass you anymore."

"I was on a date? I kind of thought we would be a couple. I'm so disappointed in my future self."

"I think it's my fault we aren't together in the future. I will always be the boy you see before you. You will live your life, growing older year by year. But in the here and now, we can be a couple, if you want."

She snuggled closer, "I would like that."

They held each other until it was too cold. Then they went up to the main house. Andri was escorted to his room by the maid. She held up a bent finger at him, "There are six security guards between you and Lilly. Don't try anything."

"I wasn't planning on anyway," he retorted.

He slept in the most comfortable bed he had ever lay on. It was morning, the sunlight streaming through the windows, before he even turned over. Getting up and stretching, he headed downstairs. The cooks were preparing breakfast.

Lilly gave him a big morning hug. The uncle frowned but said nothing as he walked by the pair.

They were all seated at the table. Heaps of food were placed in the middle. Eggs, toast, pancakes, and roasted potatoes.

"Good morning, Time God. As the guest, you are to go first."

"Thank you." Andri took a little from each platter.

"Take more, you're a growing boy," the uncle insisted.

"I am not. I won't grow an inch for the rest of eternity."

The uncle scratched his chin. "So, you will always be this size?"

"Yes."

"I see. Speaking of time travel, I wonder if you could do me a favor."

Chills went up Andri's spine.

Not waiting for an answer, the uncle went on, "If you could contact my earlier self, there is a couple of companies I should have bought long ago. If you can travel back in time and tell me about them, I would appreciate it."

"So, what? So, you can make even more money. Don't you have enough? I won't do it. I don't think I even could if I wanted to. No."

The uncle's face reddened, "Leave then. Don't eat my food or enjoy my hospitality."

Andri stood up.

"Oh, Uncle! How could you?" Lilly rushed over and threw her arms around Andri.

Andri hugged her back. Then taking a short walk out the door, he found himself in the seer pool again, going up the stairs.

"How was your visit?" Aladar asked.

"You know how my visit went. I was kicked out. That wasn't very relaxing."

"You spent time with Lilly, that was the goal. You also convinced her not to follow in the uncle's footsteps. That was a positive side effect."

"I've lost her." Andri sat down on the rim of the seer pool and put his head in his hands.

"She was always lost to you, Time God. You are not in the same timeline as she is. Relationships are hard. She will grow up and want to marry, but you'll always be this age. Enjoy the memories you've had with her. Cherish those."

Chapter Eighteen

The missions came faster after a while. Most of the travelers were gone on one errand or another. Except for Dorik and Midrel. Otherwise, Andri was alone. He wondered if he'd done something wrong or if Aladar just didn't need him anymore. The call finally came. He reported at the seer pool.

"Are you ready? I wanted to give you some time to rest, but this is important."

Andri swallowed. "I'm ready." He stepped down into the seer pool.

He stepped into the street and then back, as something passed him by. *A vehicle with wheels. Why don't they make them hover? It's a much better ride.* He scanned the area. *This is the same planet as my first mission, with a yellow sun and rolling vehicles.* He gazed up and down the street, never having seen such a crowded place. The buildings were tall enough to block out the sun. The people on the sidewalk were five across going both directions.

He stood there frozen in the moment, not knowing what to do.

"You, there. You're going to miss the bus if you don't hurry." An older woman, with her hair tied up in a bun stood over him.

"Sorry," he followed her to a big yellow school bus.

"In you go," she snapped.

He climbed up the steps then found a seat at the back of the bus.

"That's all of them," she said to the driver. "Let's go."

The door snapped closed and the bus pulled out into traffic. A girl with pig tails and a blue plaid skirt slid over a seat and asked, "Who are you? I haven't seen you before."

"I'm Andri. I usually sit up front."

"Oh, hi, I'm Ashley Morgan. What's your last name, Andri?"

He shrugged. "I only have the one name."

"Really, like Prince?"

"Like a prince, I suppose."

She giggled, "Not like a prince, silly. Like the singer. He only had one name, too. Prince."

"I've never heard of him."

"You've never heard of Prince? Are you from another planet or something?"

"Yes."

She giggled again.

The bus bumped along. Sometimes moving fast, sometimes not moving at all. Mile after mile of buildings finally thinned out and there were brief glimpses of farmland amongst all the structures. The bus came to a halt soon afterwards. Andri looked out at a large body of water.

"We're here, children. I hope you enjoyed the field trip. Your parents should be waiting for you."

The door popped open and the kids filed out.

Andri exited the bus. He saw a large two-story stone building with grass and a multicolored play set. Kids ran to cars and were hugged by waiting parents. Andri wondered what he was going to do there. *Should I have gotten on the bus?* As he looked around, his blood suddenly went cold.

Lilly's uncle opened a car door for Ashley. He walked over.

When the uncle turned around, he took a step back at the sight of Andri. "What are you doing here?"

"I could ask the same question." Andri folded his arms.

"I don't want to discuss this here. Get in, won't you, Andri?"

Ashley scooted over. "Hi, Andri, are you coming home with me?"

"It seems so." He sat down.

The uncle started the car. "Andri is a friend of mine. Ashley, how do you know him?"

"I met him on the bus. He's like from a different planet, he didn't even know who Prince was."

The uncle went pale.

Ashley whispered, "He's my stepfather, and he didn't know who Prince was either. Maybe you two are from the same planet," she giggled.

"No, we're from different planets. Neither of which has heard of Prince," Andri replied.

She giggled again.

The uncle stopped the car in front of a large house with an iron gate and a circle driveway.

"Go inside, Ashley. I want to talk to Andri for a minute."

She ran towards the door. A woman opened it up for her.

"Mom, guess what? I was at Times Square and we saw the Empire State building." Her voice faded when the door closed behind her.

The uncle put his hands on his hips. "If you mess up this deal, I swear I'll hunt you down."

"I don't know what deal you're talking about, but never threaten a Time God. They can take you down in the future, present, or past. You won't know what hit you. A Time God's revenge is a complete revenge."

The uncle took his hands off his hips and exhaled. "You're right. I shouldn't have tried to do this anyway. It's against all rules of interplanetary relationships. I've come here against my better judgement. They sent a Time God after me, after all. I know I can't win. I'm pulling up stakes and heading out."

"What about Ashley and her mother? Will they be cared for?"

"I'll leave them the house and the car and the savings account. They'll be fine."

Andri swallowed, "How's Lilly?"

"She was so mad when I told you to go, I don't think she'll ever forgive me. It's been years and she still barely talks to me."

Andri hung his head. "Years?"

"Yes, you know, you were there. She's married and has two children."

"I don't know, it's only been a few days for me."

The uncle nodded. *Was it understanding?* Andri didn't know. He sat down on a large rock near the front of the property. He watched the uncle go inside, say his goodbyes then drive away.

Andri looked around. *Why am I still here?* Andri watched the sun go down. Lights around the house came on. Soon Ashley came down and sat beside him.

"My stepfather left. He gave us the house and let mom keep her car. She cried, but she's finally done."

"Did it make you sad, too?"

She shrugged. "My daddy left, too. Mom cried then, also. She met my stepfather and was happy for a while. Now he's gone. She blames herself."

"It's not her fault. Your stepfather was using her. I don't know why, but he was."

"My grandpa owns a mining company. He's a rich man. Just because he's rich, they think my mom and me are rich, but we aren't. Its grandpa's money."

"Wait, what type of mine does he own?"

"A titanium mine."

Chapter Nineteen

Ashley's mother came out from the house. Her eyes puffy and red. "It's getting cold, you two. Come inside."

They stood up and followed her in. Inside was as beautiful as the outside. All the countertops were granite, the floors tiled, and a large chandelier hung over the dining room table.

"Do you have a place to stay?" the mother asked Andri.

"I don't. I didn't expect to be here this long."

"Where are you from?"

"A long way from here."

She put her hands on her hips. "You have singlehandedly destroyed my marriage. I want some answers at least. My husband was afraid of you. You look like a boy to me. What did you do to scare him?"

"I told him the truth. Whatever scheme he had going was wrong and he knew it. The fact that he left you and Ashley was not my doing."

The mother sighed, "It doesn't matter he's gone. I have a huge house and a car, but an empty heart. I only have three bedrooms. The third one my husband used as an exercise room. Do you mind sleeping out here on the couch?"

"That would be fine."

"Go to bed, Ashley. you have school in the morning."

"But, Mom…"

The mother pointed down the hall. Ashley slumped her shoulders but obeyed.

The mother turned back to Andri. "He called you a Time God. What does that even mean?"

"I make right the things that have gone wrong."

"So, you think whatever my husband was doing was wrong?"

Ashley shook Andri awake. "It's time for breakfast, then we have to pack lunches for school. You're coming with me because mom wants to be alone."

He stood up and stumbled to the table. He couldn't remember sleeping so poorly before. The couch looked comfortable, but it wasn't. Hard and lumpy was how he described it.

Eggs, bacon, and toast, with a glass of milk. Andri gobbled it down, then helped Ashley make sandwiches. Ashley held a finger up to her lips when her mother turned her back, took the two sandwiches from the table and put them in the pockets of her jacket. Then, when her mother turned back around, she calmly made two more. Stuck one in each lunch bag. She smiled as she handed one to Andri. "There, we're ready to go."

Ashley's mother hugged her as she headed out the door for the bus. She just sighed when Andri passed by.

He sat down next to her on the bus. "Who's the extra food for?"

"The Sullivan brothers. Their father lost his job and is drinking a lot. He doesn't make them lunches and there is no food for them to make their own."

"Is there a way I could help?"

"You already did by not telling Mom."

"Maybe we should tell someone at the school?"

"I'll tell a counselor," she nodded.

The bus rumbled to a stop and the children all climbed off.

Ashley took Andri to the office. "This is Andri, he's my cousin from down south. Is it okay if he goes with me to a couple of classes?"

"The school doesn't really have a policy on that. It's up to the individual teacher," the receptionist replied. "Meanwhile, he'll have to sign in here." She handed Andri a clip board.

"Didn't you need to talk to a counselor, Ashley?" Andri asked.

"Oh, yeah, I should do that."

"That's fine, dear," the receptionist replied. "Right this way. I see Mr. Johnson has just arrived."

Andri waited for Ashley to come back. "Mr. Johnson took the sandwiches. He will give them to the Sullivan brothers. He also said they would qualify for free lunches, so I don't need to bring them food anymore. He thanked my mother for making extra. I didn't tell him it was me. I hope he doesn't say something to her."

"That was a good thing you did."

She led him to her first class.

Was that the reason I'm here? If so, why am I not back yet?

He followed her throughout the day. All the teachers but the last one let him sit in. He spent the last period in the library.

The three of them had just sat down to dinner when the door clicked, then a man Andri didn't recognize stormed in.

"Dad, what are you doing here?"

"Grandpa," Ashley ran over and wrapped her arms around his waist. He didn't respond.

He pointed at Andri. "Is this the Time God?"

"I can speak for myself. I'm Andri."

'You cost me a lot of money."

"What are you talking about, Dad?"

"Imagine, me being in my office and this gentleman enters and asked why I'm not mining the titanium on the moon. It's ten times more plentiful there than on earth. Obviously, I point out that I can't get there. 'I can,' he responds. My first response would have been to laugh him out of my office, but he looks deadpan serious. 'Prove it.' He takes me up in a ship, has me don a space suit, not like the ones you see in the Apollo landings, but like a jogging suit with attached gloves and helmet."

The grandfather put his hands on his hips. "This creature, whatever you are, comes to town and I'm out billions of dollars. We had a deal, he was supplying the equipment and transportation, I was supplying the men and processing. We were splitting the titanium profits."

"You were planning on mining the moon?" Ashley's mother asked.

"Was it neat up there on the moon, grandpa?"

He ignored both of them and glared down at Andri. "You'd better have a spaceship, Time God."

"I do not, nor do I have access to one. The man you were dealing with isn't a good man. You are better off without him."

"I don't think so. He doesn't need to be a great guy, he just need him to get me up there. What's so intimidating about you that he would pull up stakes and leave? No worries, I'm sure you have a spaceship I can use. How did you get here?"

"Not in a spaceship. I can't help you."

Chapter Twenty

Things were still tense when Andri announced, "I'm going outside so all of you can catch up." Leaving his dinner on the table, Andri stepped out and sat on the rock by the gate. He was there a half hour when Ashley came out to join him.

"Grandpa's still yelling. He's always mad, but this could be a record." She looked Andri in the eye, "Are you some type of alien?"

"I guess you could call me that. I am part of the same galaxy as you are, and your former stepfather is. He comes from the planet I now live on, but I'm not from that planet and he doesn't live there anymore either."

"Where does my stepfather live?"

"A planet nearby. He has a mansion and servants. I visited there once, but he became angry at me, so I had to leave."

"Are all aliens like us?"

"Yes, all of them. They come in different colors, like they do here, but otherwise, we are all the same."

She stared into the night. "I want to go with you. I don't want to be here anymore. There has to be a place in the universe where I can be happy. I'm not happy here. I know I have a large home and plenty to eat. I would give that all up to be loved. I'm not loved."

Andri faced her, "Your mother, doesn't she love you?"

"She resents me. I'm the one that's preventing her from meeting the millionaire she wants to be married to and live happily ever after. She won't love him either, just his money."

"You can't come with me. If you do, you'll never age another day in your life, and your life will last forever, or until someone kills you."

"Could my stepfather help me? He was nice to me. How do I contact him?"

Andri turned back. "I'm sure you grandfather has a way to contact him. He would have given that to his business partner."

"I'll talk to him." She stood up and walked back into the house.

A few minutes later, the mother came out. "Are you here to make my life miserable? My husband left because of you, and now my daughter wants to leave." She folded her arms. "I need you to go."

He nodded, pushed the button that opened the gate and stepped through. Walking down the street, not knowing where he was going or why he was still there, a car pulled up.

"Hey, Andri, you want a ride?"

He looked over at Trevor and Augustin. Trevor sat behind the wheel. "What are you doing here?"

"Aladar said you were getting discouraged. We're here to cheer you up. Your mission's not finished yet, so keep going. Meanwhile, there's a nice diner down the street that has the best apple pie." Augustin opened the door for him. "Cadillac SUV, all the bells and whistles."

As he sat down, Andri asked, "What are you talking about?"

"It's the type of car."

Andri shook his head, "I don't like these vehicles. They don't hover. They bounce over the rough ground."

"But this is the best of the best."

"Where did you get it?"

Augustin blushed, "We, um, borrowed it. Let's not worry about that. I want some apple pie."

Doors shut, Trevor drove, a little too fast in Andri's opinion, to the diner. It was a small building sandwiched between two larger ones. A window painting announcing it was indeed a diner was the only indication of what was inside. With the car parked in front, the three of them went in.

Sitting at the bar, they ordered three apple pie slices.

A few minutes later Lilley's uncle, along with Ashley and her mother and grandfather entered.

Lilley's uncle froze when he saw Andri and the two others. "Three Time Gods! I can ignore one, but they've sent three after me. I'm leaving."

'I'm going with you," Ashley said.

"Me, too," the mom replied.

"Let's go, then." The uncle headed out the door.

Lilly's grandfather called after the group, "What makes you think they're Time Gods? they look like a group of ordinary guys to me." He stared out the door, but no one responded. "Wait for me." Turning to Andri, he said, "It took all I had to talk the man into coming back. I don't understand this Time God thing."

Augustin turned to Andri. "Looks like we're done here. Eat your pie and we'll all return together."

Andri ate his last forkful, "I'm ready when you are, but shouldn't we return the car first?"

Trevor sighed, "I suppose you're right. Even Time Gods should obey the rules."

As Andri stepped out of the seer pool, he could hear Aladin's voice. "You lost faith in me, Andri. Sometimes missions have multiple purposes."

"I'm sorry. I'm still learning."

"The school did a welfare check. The Sullivan brothers were taken out of their home and put into foster care. They grew up to be great men. One would serve as a Senator for his country. Both would be advocates for endangered children. Their father, unfortunately, drank himself to death. Both boys would have been troubled teens, if not for you.

"Ashley grew up with her mother and stepfather at his mansion on Anderia. She would come back to earth as the first interstellar delegate, after earth finally realizes they are not alone in the universe.

"You saved her grandfather from his own stupidity. He would've started the mining company on the moon. A tractor would have smashed into a worker's dormitory and seventeen men would have died. It would be then that the nations would find out he was mining the moon. After the lawsuits and government involvement, he would have ended up bankrupt."

"Thank you for telling me that and sending Trevor and Agustin to help me."

"I had to. Those two men were planning on going ahead with the mining project, despite you. It took two more Time Gods to convinced them."

Chapter Twenty-One

Only two suns hung over the horizon as Andri sat on the edge of the inland sea beach Listening as the waves splashed against the shore, his heart felt heavy, troubled about all the things happening to him. He never wanted to become a Time God. He had helped people, it was true, but he had also killed. A shudder went down his spine. *How can I be done? How can I go back to my home planet and farm like my father did, and his father before him?* It was all he wanted to do.

A woman and three young girls sat on the beach a few paces away. The girls started digging in the sand. The beginnings of a rough looking sandcastle emerged. After a while, the woman made eye contact and smiled. She moved to sit beside Andri.

"Andri, you haven't aged a day in all these years."

He gasped. "Lilly?"

"I'm not the fourteen-year-old you remember, but yes, it's me." She hugged him. "It does seem like yesterday I met you for the first time. Come, let's show my girls how to build a proper sandcastle."

"It was yesterday to me." He knelt in the sand.

Straightening up the walls, Andri and Lilly helped the children build the castle. It wasn't the masterpiece of ages past, but it satisfied the little girls.

"You still come here after all this time?" Lilly asked.

"Just to sit and remember the past. I really fell for you. The other Time Gods warned me it wouldn't work out, but I didn't listen. Sometimes, I step into the seer pool and come to the past, just to be with you again."

"You did visit me a lot back in those days. I fell for you, too," she kissed him on the cheek.

"Where's your husband?"

Her face darkened. "Anderia was under attack. The planet Tescire invaded. My uncle talked my husband into fighting for the freedom of Anderia. He was killed. I had so hoped the Time Gods would intervene, but they did nothing."

"I'm so sorry. We don't pick our assignments. They're given to us."

"It's in the past. We can't change it." She took a deep breath. "So, how have you been?"

"I was just here contemplating my life. I've killed people, I've been in wars, and traveled all over. I'm the same age I was years ago. I wish I'd never been made a Time God."

"Have you helped people, though?"

He gazed down at the sand. "Yes, you're right. I've helped many. I should look at the good I do and not the bad."

"That's how you get through the bad parts, by focusing on the good." She rubbed his shoulders. "You're a mighty man in my eyes."

"Thank you."

She stood up. "I've got to get the girls under shelter. A third sun will rise soon, and it will be too hot for them out here. I guess I'll see you in another few years."

When he stood up and she hugged him. "Goodbye, Lilly."

"Let's not say goodbye, let's say, 'See you later'."
She waved and walked away, holding the littlest one's hand.

Walking back to the compound, Andri paused by
the seer pool. "Why didn't we help Anderia?"

Aladar's voice went soft, "It was a trap. Tescire
wanted to draw the Time Gods out and destroy us. That's
why they invaded. Many volunteers rushed to the aid of
Anderia. Tescire was driven back with heavy losses. We
didn't need to respond. Buliston was our answer to
Tescire's demand that they have one of their own compete
to be a Time God. If he would have been made one, he
would have done his own missions to help his home
planet's agenda. There was no way we would have allowed
that. That's when the time bandits were formed by them.
Tescire wants to control the galaxy."

"Lilly's husband was killed."

"Yes, his patrol was ambushed at a place called
Allac Hern."

"I want to save him."

Andri waited for an answer. It took a long time for
her to respond. Finally, she said, "I will allow it. Normally
I do not grant personal missions, but you are not doing it
for yourself. It will be a difficult task for someone your
age. If you fail, I will not send anyone to save you."

Andri swallowed. "I'm okay with that."

"Then step into the seer pool."

Holding his breath, he stepped forward.

Night had fallen. Andri looked around, he could see
men sneaking through the brush and setting up positions.

Along a trail, in the distance, he could see a patrol slowly
making their way through the forest.

I have a gun. Aladar thought of everything. He
pointed it at the nearest Tescire warrior and pulled the
trigger. The man slumped down. Andri dove into a bush
then crawled out the other side. Energy weapons blasted the
area where Andri just was. He crawled away faster. When
he had gone several yards, he peeked out between two
trees. The patrol had stopped and was fanning out. The
Tescire soldiers retreated in the confusion.

Andri breathed a sigh of relief. It was short-lived. In
the next instant, a gun jammed against his back.

"Drop the weapon or I'll blast you."

Andri dropped the gun. The man tied Andri's hands
behind his back and pushed him down the trail toward the
patrol.

"Captain, I caught this one in the woods with a
weapon, waiting for us."

The captain's eyes widened. "Well, well, well, what
do we have here? I know who you are. My wife has a
picture of you by her nightstand." He turned to his man.
"Untie him."

"But, Sir…"

"Don't you recognize your Time Gods? I know this
one especially. What are you doing here, Andri?"

Andri didn't answer but waited for the man to untie
him. Then he rubbed his wrists.

The captain asked his men, "Did you see any dead
Tescire up there?"

"There was one, Sir."

"You caused the ruckus up there, didn't you, Andri? You saved us from being ambushed. Whose idea was this mission of yours?"

"It was mine." Andri swallowed. "When I saw Lilly with her three little girls, it made me sad. I had to come back in time and save you."

"Three little girls? I only have two."

"Then she hasn't told you yet."

He held out his hand to one of his men. "Give me that communicator."

The man handed him a box with a dish antenna. It buzzed. "Honey, I just called to tell you I'm all right. Say, I heard through the grapevine that you were pregnant. Is that true?"

"Who told you? I was going to surprise you with the news when you returned."

"Andri told me. He just saved my life."

She screeched, "Andri's there? You would have died? I need you back here now."

"I'll see you soon enough. The fighting is wrapping up." The captain hung up the phone. "So why did you do it? When I proposed to my wife you know what she told me? She said, 'I'll marry you, but my heart will always belong to Andri.'"

"I'm a sixteen-year-old boy. I'll always be a sixteen-year-old boy. Last time I saw Lilly, she was a grown woman with three children. I'm not your competition."

The captain stuck out his hand. "Thank you for my life."

Andri shook it. "I have to leave now." The captain nodded as Andri headed down the trail.

When he stepped out of the seer pool, Aladar said, "It was a good thing you did today Andri."

Chapter Twenty-Two

Andri found himself in a green field. In the distance, he could hear someone talking. A group of men sat close to a cliff of broken dark grey rocks, listening. They sported long beards and hair. Each covered against the morning chill with jackets of furs. In the valley below, he could see tents of animal skin with people milling nearby.

"Hello."

Andri turned to see a girl, about his age, standing at his elbow.

"Hello," he responded. "What's going on?"

"Don't you know?" Her forehead creased. "That's the Althing meeting. They're going over the law and settling disputes." She pointed at a rocky outcropping. "The Lawspeaker is reading the law."

"Oh?"

"Why did you come all this way and not know that?"

"I was brought here. I didn't know why."

She smiled. "Oh. What clan are you?"

He swallowed. "Um, the one just south of here."

"Sturlungar?"

"Yes, that's it."

She shook her head. "I'm from Sturlungar. You're not." Grabbing his hand, she said, "Come, I have something to show you."

He followed her up the hill. There, just down from a waterfall was a large pond. Behind him he could see a green valley with a river running through it culminating in a blue water lake.

"This is the drowning pool. They killed my mother here. My father is a chieftain. He said she committed infanticide." She shook her head, "She was a midwife. The child was stillborn, she didn't kill it. My father wanted a younger wife, so he had my mother drowned in the pool here. Come, I have more to show you." She pulled him towards the waterfall.

They climbed over boulders, up to the top of the waterfall and the edge of the cliff. "Here, look into the pool."

He gazed down at a small puddle between two rocks. He could see her reflection in the puddle, but not his own.

"That's what I thought. She held up a small, handheld object and pushed the red button it had in the middle. A green, translucent dome encapsulated them.

"What have you done?"

"The men from the sky said you would come to rescue me. My father beats me, and they said the next time he was drunk, he would beat me to death. He's down there drinking heavily right now. They said you would come and you wouldn't have a reflection in the pool. The men from the sky said they are going to get rid of my father and give me a chest full of gold so I can live well for the rest of my life."

He touched the dome. Sparks flew off the dome where his finger touched. "Ow." He pulled it back. The tip was black. *Time bandits!*

Five men walked towards the dome, smiles on their faces. "Well, what have we here? We caught the little Time God." They dropped a heavy chest just outside the dome. "Here's your pay, missy. We spiked your father's ale. If he drinks much more, he'll die."

"My name's not missy. My name's Freyja. Let me out of here."

"Well, Time God, you're in a pickle. Your buddies can neither see nor hear you while you're under the dome. On the count of three, Missy, you run out and we'll run in. One, two, three."

The dome went off, Freya ran out and two of the time bandits, dressed as Vikings, ran in. They caught Andri, who was also attempting to run out, and pulled him back just as the dome reappeared.

Andri, for his part, was having none of it. He bit the one on his left until the man let go of his grip. The other, he punched in the gut with his free hand. The man doubled over. A quick right to the jaw sent that one to the ground.

The dome turned off and the other three rushed in. Two of them grabbed Andri's arms, while a third one punched him repeatedly in the gut.

"Don't hurt him," Freyja pleaded. "You said you wouldn't hurt him."

"You fools, turn the dome back on," the man on the ground yelled.

They stopped to look for the sensor with the button. It was too late. A blast took out the one beating Andri. The ones holding him only made it a step or two before they dropped as well. The man who'd been bitten reached for a weapon, but he died before he could pull it out of his belt.

Agustin and Trevor stood up, along with three other Time Gods, and walked over. The time bandit on the ground raised his hands.

Agustin looked down at him, then pulled an energy weapon out of his fur coat. "You, I'm going to let live. You tell your leader to stop this stupidity or we'll be going after him next."

The time bandit nodded.

All of the dead time bandits were disarmed so no trace of the future could be found on them.

"Aladar, get us out of here," Trevor said.

"My father! He's coming up the cliff!" Freyja gasped.

Augustin and Trevor assisted Andri out of the seer pool. He could barely walk, the pain in his gut hurt so much.

"What is this place?"

They turned to see Freyja standing up. "I'm not wet? What's going on?"

"What's she doing here?" Augustin asked.

Aladar's voice replied, "I couldn't let her die. You were leaving, so I brought her with you."

"But, now, she's a Time God."

"Yes, that is the way of things. Put her in the room across from Andri."

Freyja scanned the room back and forth. "I hear a voice, but there's no one there. Where am I?"

Still doubled over, Andri sat on the edge of the pool. "You are somewhere your father can't hurt you."

"Follow me." Trevor took her hand. As soon as they neared the steel door, it opened.

"Ahh," she stepped back.

"You can't be so skittish. You're in the future where everything is automatic. Watch this. 'Lights.'"

The hallway lit up. Her eyes widened.

"Follow me."

She walked slowly after him, checking everything out as she went.

Trevor stood in front of her door. "Open, turn on lights." The room lit up. "Commands respond to this voice only," He turned to her. "Say something."

"What?"

"That'll do. Go ahead on in. This is your room. Dinner is in an hour. It will be at the end of the hall. Make yourself at home."

She took an uneasy step inside. The door closed behind her. He heard a screech as it closed.

Chapter Twenty-Three

Andri heard banging on Freyja's door as he passed by on his way to dinner. His stomach still hurt, but he was hungry after his trauma. He stood there for a minute, then said, "Intercom, what's going on in there?"

"I'm stuck. I can't get out."

"Say, 'open'."

"Open!" She rushed out as soon as the door did.

"What's going on?" She hid behind him.

"It only responds to your voice. I'll help you. You can say lights off, open, close, or lights on."

"Lights off." The lights in her room went off. "Close." She stood there wide-eyed.

"You ready to go to dinner?"

She nodded, so Andri led the way.

At dinner, Dorik had made something special for her so she would feel at home.

When he put it in front of her, she stared at it. "What is it?"

"It's lasagna, a dish from your planet."

"My planet? What do you mean by that?"

His face reddened. "I'm sorry, what do you eat?"

She looked around the room, "What's going on?"

"Fair enough," Andri said. "You've stepped into the seer pool. You will never age another day in your life. You think that's a good thing, but trust me, it isn't. You are no longer on the same planet you're from. You are many, many light-years away in fact. Before you get angry with us, you would be dead right now if we hadn't saved you."

He took a forkful of his dinner. "You should try this. It's very good."

She stood up. "I don't understand. This can't be happening."

Derik put a hand on her shoulder. "It will be okay. Sit and eat."

Sitting back down, she took a deep breath and tasted her dinner. Nodding, she said, "It's good."

"Maybe you two can go up to the surface today, and Andri can show you the inland sea. You're about the same age. You could be friends."

Andri finished the last bite of his dinner and wiped his lips. "We can't ever be friends. She betrayed me." He stood up and walked out.

Freyja burst into tears and rushed down the hall. She passed Andri, yelling, "Open," when she was close to her room. "Close hard," she said as she entered. The door closed with a pop.

Andri shrugged and went into his room. A few minutes later there was a ring at his door. "Open."

Augustin, Trevor, and Derik entered. Derik held out some cake. "I thought I'd try to soften you up."

"I didn't do anything wrong," Andri replied.

"You don't have to be wrong to be wrong," Augustin replied. "I mean with women, that is."

"What does that even mean?" Andri asked.

"I guess," Trevor added, "what he really meant to say is, we are going to be around a long time and you not talking to her means she won't talk to us and it's going to be really uncomfortable around here for, well, a very long time. Can you try to get along with her? Maybe, take her to the surface and show her around?"

"I don't want to."

Trevor shook his head. "We didn't ask you if you wanted to, we asked you to do it. I think it will be better for all of us if we get along. If you can't do it for yourself, do it for us."

"Why don't you do it?" Andri asked.

"I'm not the one who hurt her feelings."

"She turned me over to the time bandits!"

"I'm sure she's sorry. She was going to die that day. It wasn't anything personal."

"I'll think about it," Andri conceded.

"Good, think about it fast. She's still holed up in her room,' Trevor replied. The three of them left.

A few minutes later Andri sighed heavily, then stood up and entered the hall. He rang Freyja's bell. There was no answer, so he knocked.

"What?" came her voice through the door.

"I want to talk. It's Andri."

Freyja stared at him with a red face and bloodshot eyes. "Oh, it's you."

"I said it was Andri."

"I don't know who's who, I just met you all. Now you've kidnapped me."

"We didn't kidnap you. We saved you."

"If that's what you want to call it. I'm a prisoner here. I can't get out."

"You're not a prisoner. You can come and go as you please. Let me show you how to do that."

She followed him into the room with the seer pool. "What is this place? I didn't get wet when I was in the water there."

"It's not water. It's the seer pool. We can go anywhere in history using that. But not today. At the end of this corridor is a door that leads out to the planet you're on."

"You keep talking about planets. There is only one planet, except for the moon and that's only a big rock."

Andri sighed heavily. "Follow me."

At the end of the tunnel, he placed his hand on the pad. The stone door open and they stepped out.

"There aren't two suns. That's impossible," she folded her arms. "What type of trick are you trying to play on me?"

"You aren't on the planet of your birth, but you are right, there are not two suns. This planet has six. It never gets dark here."

The hover bus drove by while he talked. She gasped.

"Yes, and there are no horse-drawn carts here either. It's all mechanized. We must go back soon. A third sun is about to rise and it will be too hot for us to be on the surface." He put his hand on the pad, and the door opened, then they stepped inside.

She passed as the neared the seer pool. "I want to go back to my home."

"You won't recognize it. Your father died centuries ago. There are no more Vikings, only their descendants."

"Please."

He shrugged, "Okay." He led her into the seer pool.

They arrived back at the drowning pool. She turned to see tour buses and cars lined up. "What's going on? What are those things?"

"The same things you saw before only these ride on the ground and do not hover over it."

"And that building down in the valley?"

He gazed at what where she pointed. "That's a church."

Tears filled her eyes. "It's all so different. What happened to me?"

"You stepped in the seer pool. Your life will never be the same."

"Take me back."

"I warned you."

"You don't need to make me feel bad. I already do."

He ignored her. "Aladar, we are ready.'

When she stepped out of the seer pool, she walked straight to her room and closed the door.

Trevor smiled at Andri, "How did it go?"

"I made things worse. She hates me even more now." Andri didn't wait for an answer but hid in his room also.

Chapter Twenty-Four

The balloons drifted back and forth in the light breeze as Lilly blew out the birthday cake candles, sixteen of them. Andri clapped with joy at seeing her so happy. This was the best and the worst day of his life. He was delighted at being there, but also knew he would soon have to say goodbye.

She opened each present, saving Andri's for last. The unwrapped hover scooter was the easiest to guess, under its purple bow. A sweater and a new swimsuit were some of the others. The small box was next. She opened it and pulled out a ring, a simple silver band with runes on it.

"It's a friendship ring. An Earth tradition," he smiled.

"Earth? I've never heard of that planet."

"They're backward, not part of any league of planets. They barely venture into space. Those are Viking runes. Viking are a warrior race. The men sleep sitting up with a weapon within their reach, so they can defend themselves in case they're attacked during the night."

She slipped it on her finger and held it up to the light. "It's beautiful." She hugged him.

When the third sun began its rise over the horizon, the party-goers left in droves. Lilly's mom urged her to hurry. She threw her arms around Andri's neck. "I don't want this to end." She kissed him long and hard. "I've got to go. Do you need a ride anywhere? I'd like to try out my new scooter."

He laughed. "No, but thanks. The door is just around the corner."

Her smile disappeared. "Will I ever see you again?"

"Yes, we'll meet many times over the years."

She teared up. "It must be hard for you seeing the future and the past." She hugged him again. "I've got to go. It's getting too hot."

"I love you." It would be the last time he saw her. He often thought about her, maybe going back in time and visiting her the younger her, but he never did. It hurt too much.

She waved as she turned to join her mother.

As Andri stepped out of the seer pool, Freyja was sitting next to it. "Was that your girlfriend?"

"What?"

"I watched you kiss her. Is that your girlfriend? It is isn't it?"

Andri sat down beside Freyja. "She's married to someone else and has four kids. The last one, a boy, they named after me."

"She's only a girl."

"I went back in time to see her. We can go back in time too. I loved her, but I'm just frustrating myself visiting her. She grew older and I stayed a boy. You will never age, either."

"I tell myself it isn't possible, but I watch the pool and see the people coming and going. It's happening anyway, the impossible, that is."

"I told her goodbye tonight. I won't visit her again, even though she won't know it as I have visited her in the future a few times. It's just too hard knowing that, no matter how much she loves me, we won't go any further than the kiss I had today."

"I want to see my mother. I want to see her when she's young and full of energy. When she married my father, he ruled over her with an iron fist. She was always sad with him around."

"Go, then."

She shook her head. "I'm afraid. Will you come with me?"

"Can I trust you? You turned me over to the time bandits last time."

"I'm sorry. I didn't know any better. I believed their lies. I won't ever do that again."

"You're a traveler now, too. They will want to capture you as much as they wanted to capture me."

Her eyes met his. "Please come with me."

"I'll show you how it's done. You have to think of the date, time, and place while you enter into the seer pool"

He stepped in and she clung to his hand. "I've got it."

"Brr," Andri said when he found himself knee-deep in snow.

"We changed clothes." Freyja looked down at the furs on her.

"Aladar takes care of us. She makes sure we have what we need to survive."

A woman with a basket walked out of the stone hut.

"Mother!" Freyja called out.

"Freyja, what are you doing out here? I just left you in the house."

"Mother!" Freyja rushed to her arms.

"Are you okay? How did you get outside so fast?"

A bearded man peeked out. "Hurry up so you can get back. I want my supper."

"Yes, dear."

Freyja glared at the man, "Mur…"

Andri clapped his hand over Freyja's mouth. "Stop, you're going to mess everything up. Aladar, get us out of here."

As they stepped out of the pool, Freyja slumped down. "It made it worse. I saw him, too." She put her face in her hands and sobbed.

Andri rubbed her back. "I've never gone back to see my mother for that reason. It would only make me sadder that I'm not with her."

She wrapped her arms around his neck and sobbed for a minute. Red-faced, she sat up. "I'm sorry, I got your shoulder all wet. I'm going to my room."

"Don't do that. You shouldn't be alone right now. Let's go find some food."

They headed down the hall. Several of the travelers were there eating. Andri picked up two plates of cake and ice cream. "These are a treat from your planet, only maybe not from when you lived."

She took a spoonful. "It's good. You keep talking about my planet. Did you come from here?"

"No, I lived on a farming planet. We supplied food to a lot of other planets."

"You were a farmer then?"

"I would have been if I had stayed. That was the life I had planned to live. Now I'm here helping others."

"Do you like it here?"

"Mostly. I have friends here. I would have been perfectly happy growing old as a farmer, and even growing old with Lilly by my side, but that is not my lot in life."

She patted his arm. "I am grateful to you for saving my life."

Chapter Twenty-Five

When Andri arrived at the seer pool, Freyja was sitting on the edge of it. "Good morning," he said even though he had no idea whether it was morning or afternoon. The planet was always light, but that didn't matter. He couldn't see the suns from down below the rock anyway.

"Hi, I get to go with you," she smiled.

"I'm going on a mission. You can't come this time."

"Aladar said this was my first mission and I was to go with you when you came." She folded her arms.

"But…"

Andri stopped when Aladar's voice said, "Take the girl. Tell everyone she's your twin sister. This mission requires both of you."

Andri sighed. "Well, come on, then."

She smiled and held his hand.

"We don't have to hold hands. We'll end up in the same place."

She frowned. "I'm just making sure."

"This is such a cute dress." Freyja looked down on the pink with blue stripes fabric. Then she gazed about. "Where is this place?"

Andri pulled his hand back, then scanned the area, seeing a large sand desert around them, two moons in the sky, one of which had a blue tint to it. "The planet Amadore."

Soon a large transport landed next to them. Freyja squeaked and stepped back behind Andri.

Square, with rust-stained silver sides, it had two large engines that gave it the ability to take off and land vertically. An old man with a weather-stained tan cap stepped out. "You can't be standing here in the desert-like this. The sun will kill you, if you survive the sand creatures that is. I'm Orand."

"Thank you for stopping for us, I'm Andri and this is…" He paused.

"I know who you are, Time God. Who's that with you?"

"I'm Freyja," she shook the man's hand.

"Well, well, what brings you here?"

Andri answered, "She's a Time God, also. She's here to help me. How can we be of service?"

"Come, step in here before the sand creatures wake up from their daily nap."

When the door closed, Orand took the controls to the ship. Lifting off, he said, "A female Time God. I never thought the mistress of the temple would allow that."

"She didn't. It was an accident," Andri replied.

"Well, welcome to Amadore, Freyja. We'll be in the city in a few minutes. Not to worry."

"Thank you, Orand."

Inside the ship were bare pipes leading up to the engines. Heat radiated from them. Boxes and tools were scattered around. There was nowhere to sit except for the boxes.

Freyja grabbed a rag from the floor and wiped off one of the dirty side windows so she could see out. Desert spread out in every direction. Soon, a large city came into view, with transports, like the one they were in, taking off and landing, coming in from all directions.

Orand brought the ship in for a landing. It seemed to Andri to be one of the dingier parts of town.

Orand picked up a microphone. "Orand in the Delsus reporting in. I've landed at pad 5592, oh, and I have two Time Gods with me."

"Two Time Gods? We only need one. Why did you pick them up? I dispatched a transport a few minutes ago. They would have been a lot happier in that than in your scow."

Orand frowned. "Nevertheless, I've got them, come and get 'em."

He hung the mike up. "Scow? He called ol' Delsus a scow."

"Thank you for bringing us into the city, Orand," Freyja gave him a bow.

A few minutes later a long black hovercar pulled up. The driver, in a tuxedo, stepped out and opened the back door. A woman, in a light blue dress with pearls sewn along the edges, stepped out.

"I am princess Eyana." She smiled, "I will escort you to the president."

Freyja whispered into Andri's ear. "A real princess is escorting me."

He whispered back, "The more pomp and ceremony a task has, the more they will be asking us to do."

"Oh," Freyja replied, but stepped in the vehicle anyway.

The ride took over an hour. Freyja spent the whole time, wide-eyed and talking to the princess.

The car stopped in front of a large building with columns and a white marble façade. Andri and Freyja stepped out when the driver opened the door.

"We have nothing like this in Iceland," Freyja commented.

A man, in a blue suit with a flower in the lapel came down the steps to them. "I am Ivar, the secretary to the president. Please, follow me."

He walked them up the steps, into an elevator that took them several floors up. When they exited, a marble hallway with the crest of the planet on the floor led to double ornate wood doors. Ivar opened the doors and led them in.

The president sat at a large dark-wood desk. "Andri, welcome. I told them to send their best and they sent you. Please sit." He motioned them to two seats in front of the desk. "And you are the other Time God. I didn't remember there being new Time God trials recently. Perhaps I was busy with the affairs of state and missed it."

"I'm Freyja." She took a seat.

"You see," the president began, "The Tescire are giving us trouble. They have mined out all the natural resources of their planet and have tried but failed to capture nearby planets, those that still have their natural resources, including yours, Andri, I believe. Their game now is sending out ships to pirate freighters of the trade alliance. We want to know what the Time Gods intend to do about it." The president sat back in his chair.

"I will take your concerns to our leaders," Andri replied. "The Tescire have also tried to take over the Time Gods. They almost captured one of us recently." He glanced over to Freyja, who shrunk down in her chair. "But we were able to stop them. We have never come in the middle of a dispute between planets, however, and I doubt we will now."

"Something needs to be done or I will end my support for the Time Gods."

Andri glared at him. "Your people have benefited greatly over the years because the Time Gods have come to the rescue of thousands of them. It would be sad if we told them we would never be back."

The president swallowed. "Well, let's not be hasty. Just deliver my message and I will await a response."

Andri stood up, bowed, then made his way out the door. Freyja rushed to keep up. At the bottom of the steps, a hovercar waited for them, but Andri waved it off. "We will make our own way back," he told the driver.

"You are a boy, " Freyja scolded. "You can't be talking to presidents like that."

"He's bluffing. He can't solve his own problems, so he wants us to solve them for him. He doesn't send any support for the Time Gods anyway. This is Trevor's planet to deal with. The only reason I have this mission is because Trevor has no diplomatic skills at all."

She patted his arm. "It's okay. We had fun here today. We'll have stories to tell the grandkids."

He looked at her sideways. "Grandkids?"

As they stepped out of the seer pool, Aladar's voice said, "Well done, Andri and Freyja. They will form a league of planets soon to blast the Tescires out of the sky.

All they needed to know was we were not going to solve their problems for them."

Andri walked to his room leaving Freyja alone.

Chapter Twenty-Six

When Andri arrived at the lunchroom the next day, a group of travelers were gathered around Freyja listening to her tell about meeting the princess. Andri ignored them. Picking up his food, he sat at the end of the table, away from the group.

Trevor came down and sat beside him. "She's a hoot."

"If you say so." Andri took another forkful of his lunch.

"You really do need to get over this 'She betrayed me,' thing. She's one of us, and we need to stick together."

"She didn't have to go through the trials. Aladar brought her back with a split-second decision."

"I didn't go through the trials, either. I was the fifth traveler. It wasn't until recently that they've done the trials. It isn't to select a traveler, either; you were selected before the trails began. It's so the people have some entertainment and feel a part of the process."

Andri looked up. "You mean I went through that for nothing?"

"No, it builds character and, boy, did you need some."

Andri rolled his eyes. Later on that day as he read in his room, Aladar's voice said, "It is time for you to head down to the seer pool. Freyja is waiting for you there."

"Why? I can do this alone."

"Someday you'll thank me for her help. For now, she comes from a backward society that rode horses and believed they were alone in the universe. She needs to learn about the galaxy. She needs to learn it from you."

He sighed, and headed down to the seer pool.

When he arrived, she grabbed his hand in hers., "Let's go."

"We don't have to hold hands. We'll arrive at the same place anyway."

She held a finger to her lips, "Shh."

He sighed but walked into the pool.

"What planet is this?" She gazed up in wonderment at the lights on the tower in front of her. Street vendors lined the sidewalks. Each offered the same items as the one next to them. A bridge separated them from the tower. Tour boats sailed under it.

"This is your planet." He slipped his hand away when she relaxed her grip.

She scowled. "My planet has nothing like this."

"Not when and where you lived. This is a country called France. That's the Eifel Tower. Since I keep getting sent back to this planet over and over again, I've read a lot about it."

"Can we climb it?" She clasped her hands together. "I see stairs."

"No, we need to figure out why we're here."

"You don't know what we're supposed to be doing?" her forehead creased.

"I never know."

"Then our mission could start from up there?" She pointed to the top of the Eifle Tower.

He shrugged. "It could, I guess."

"Then let's go." She grabbed his hand and pulled him toward the tower.

A booth stood between them and the path to the tower. The lady there said, "Please take everything out of your pockets and go through the metal detector."

"I don't have anything in my pockets."

"Proceed."

She stepped tentatively through the detector. A man on the other side motioned her forward. Andri took a card out of his pocket, then stepped through himself. He didn't set it off either. He grabbed his card back.

"What do you suppose that was?"

"They want to make sure you don't have any weapons. They worry about terrorists in this day and age."

"What's a terrorist?"

"Someone who kills and destroys to terrorize an entire population for political gain."

"Oh," she walked under the tower and looked up. It was a gridwork of iron going in all directions. "Wow." She spun slowly around eyeing every detail. "I never knew something like this existed."

She trotted over to them. He followed. They saved their breath for the climb, not speaking. They arrived at the first level, but it wasn't good enough for Freyja. She beckoned him further.

When they reached the second level, he held up his hand. "Six hundred and eighty steps, that's my daily limit."

She gave him a sideways glance, "Really?"

"Actually, it's way past my daily limit. I'm going to enjoy the view from here."

The city of Paris spread out in all directions. Boulevards, large government buildings, and apartment buildings were in stretched out before them.

"So many lights." Her eyes sparkled.

A man in a dark coat passed them. Andri followed him with his eyes.

She shivered. "He's up to no good."

"Are you sure?"

"I can feel his evil intent."

Andri turned and followed the man at a distance.

Then man ducked around a corner and pulled out grey material from around his waist. He formed it into a shape that fit through the block fencing that surrounded the second platform. He placed a wire in the grey object, then rushed to the fence and pushed it through.

"Bomb!" Andri yelled, as the man pulled a detonator out of his pocket. Andri tackled him. The man reached to push the button, but Freyja snatched it out of his hand.

The man struggled with Andri's iron grip. Other people came to hold the man down. Soon sirens interrupted the quiet. Dozens of police cars pulled up to the tower and officers ran up the stairs, not waiting for the elevator. They handcuffed the man and led him away.

A police officer came up to Andri and Freyja. "You have the thanks of all France for your actions today. The bomb stuck on the edge of the tower. It didn't make it all the way to the ground. It wouldn't have brought down the tower but would have rained debris on all those below. Dozens would have been killed and injured. The president of France wants to personally thank you. There are hundreds of newspaper reporters down at the bottom, who want to talk to you also." He spoke into a box on his shoulder. "I'll be right back to take you to the president."

"Now would be a good time, Aladar."

Freyja found herself walking out of the seer pool. "Wait, we were going to meet the president of France."

"We don't want the time bandits finding out where we were or what we've done. We need to avoid the spotlight," Andri said it convincingly, even though he wasn't convinced himself.

Freyja sighed and walked off towards her room.

"Well?" Aladar's voice said.

"You were right. She has an awareness that I lack. I would have let that man walk past me. Dozens would have been hurt. I will no longer complain when you pair the two of us together."

"You'll make a good Time God one of these days, Andri."

Chapter Twenty-Seven

At the lunchroom, a crowd of men gathered around Freyja as she related the heroics of her last adventure.

Andri sat by himself eating soup. Trevor walked up. "You can join the party. She's telling us what a great hero you are."

Andri smiled. "The telling is so much more than the actual events. That girl can spin a yarn. What she fails to mention is her part in this story."

"I still need you to like her."

Andri looked over. "She's growing on me."

The smile disappeared off Trevor's face. "We have a problem. We found out the leader of the time bandits is a former Time God. He was doing evil things to get gain, so Aladar refused to bring him back to the seer pool. That's why he isn't going away after a generation. He's one of us. He doesn't age. One of these days, you, me, and Augustin will have to go after him."

"We need to take Freyja with us. She has a way of reading people. We'll need her help."

"Well." Trevor took a step back. "I never thought you'd say something like that."

"Like I said, she's growing on me."

Trevor, Augustin, Freyja, and Andri stood by the seer pool. Freyja instinctively took Andri's hand. He didn't resist.

Aladar's voice said, "Not this time, Freyja. He's going to a different place than you."

Freyja let go. "I thought we were on this mission together?"

"You are, but I'm setting you down in different places. In case one of you gets caught, the others can save them."

The group proceeded into the seer pool.

No sooner had Andri hit the ground than he felt the barrel of a weapon pressed into his back. "Walk into that doorway," a gruff voice ordered.

Andri did as told. A tall man, with well-kept hair wearing a tuxedo sat in a chair facing the door. "Andri. Welcome to Rome. I love this city of fashion. I can wear fancy clothes around town and nobody even bats an eye."

Andri stiffened. "Who are you?"

"I am one of you. Well, it was before you were one of you. Your friends Trevor and Augustin will recognize me. They will be joining us soon. I am Gabranth."

"How did you know where I'd be?"

"I can't give you my secrets." He smiled. "Never mind, I can since you won't live long enough to report back to Aladar. I set sensors around the temple of the rock to record when you go to and from the seer pool. You see, I didn't plan to take the pool by force, or I would have sent more men. I want to control the Time Gods, not destroy them. I know Trevor and Augustin are here. I'm having my men track them down as we speak."

"You can't control us by killing us."

Gabranth chuckled, "I'm only going to kill you. You see, you killed my dear friend when you climbed that cliff and shot down into the temple grounds. I want revenge. With Trevor and Augustin, I figure, with enough torture, they will eventually come around. The last time I tortured a Time God, I didn't have the technology to block Aladar from seeing what I was doing. This time around, I do. The house is shielded from her view."

Andri turned as the door opened. Trevor and Augustin were pushed into the room, their faces bruised and bleeding, their hands tied behind their back.

"These two gave us trouble, boss, but we persuaded them." They forced Trevor and Augustin to sit in the corner.

Gabranth stood up. "I've got to go. Kill that one slowly," he pointed at Andri, "bring the others to our headquarters as soon as night falls."

"Yes, boss."

Gabranth walked out the door.

The taller of the two men set his gaze on Andri. "How should we do it? Painfully, I suppose."

"We shoot him, starting with his feet, then work up his legs and arms. Let him sit bleeding for hours, then finish him off."

"I like that plan," the tall one pulled out his energy weapon.

Andri swallowed involuntarily. A knock came on the door.

"The boss back already?" The tall one opened, only to find Freyja standing there.

"Please, Sir, I'm lost. Can you tell me where the Coliseum is? I was supposed to meet my parents there, but I seem to be going in the wrong direction."

He pointed down the street. "That way. Now get out of here."

In a quick motion, she wrestled the weapon out of his hand and aimed it at him.

"Now, don't do anything rash, girl."

The shorter man laughed. "She won't shoot you. She's just playing with you, fool."

The room lit up as the gun went off, then lit up again. The two men lay dead on the floor.

"I didn't mean to kill them. I saw them take Trevor and Augustin. I was around the corner. They didn't see me. He wasn't paying attention, so I grabbed his gun. I hope I didn't do anything wrong." She gasped, "What have I done?"

"Cut these bands off of us," Trevor said.

She cut Andri's off first. He hugged her. "You did great. There are two less bad guys in the galaxy because of you."

Andri and Freyja cut Trevor and Augustin's bands off.

"We should go after Gabranth," Andri said.

"He's many miles away by now. No, we cut our losses, but before we go, we find this energy field that blinds Aladar. We can defeat it if we do."

An hour later, they had found all the devices and disabled them. "Aladar, we're ready to go home."

As they stepped out of the seer pool, Aladar's voice said, "We've found his sensors that were tracking our movement. He doesn't know about Freyja. That is to our advantage."

Andri hugged her again. "Thanks for saving my life."

She smiled. "Thanks for letting me go with you. I heard you even asked that I should come. Am I forgiven for betraying you?"

"A million times over."

Chapter Twenty-Eight

"I've found Gabranth. He's up the coast in La Spezia, Italy. Do you want me to send someone else after him?" Aladar's voice said.

Andri rose., "No, I want to go after him."

"I'll send Augustin and Trevor with you."

"I want Freyja, also."

"Of course."

The others were waiting when he arrived at the seer pool.

"Are we going to be together, or are you going to put us in different spots like last time?" Freyja asked.

"All together this time," Aladar replied.

Freyja grabbed Andri's hand, "Okay, I'm ready."

He didn't resist.

Gabranth sat on an umbrella chair by the seashore. He didn't look up when Andri sat next to him.

"How are you doing today?" Andri asked.

Almost spilling his drink when he saw Andri, Gabranth tried to stand up, but Augustin and Trevor put their hands on his shoulders and forced him back in his chair.

"You can't run. Aladar will bring you back from wherever you go. We have you now. A cell has been constructed just for you, in the tunnels under the temple of the rock. You'll spend the rest of eternity locked up."

Gabranth reached down and pulled up a small metallic cylinder from the rocky beach. "They turned off my sensor shield. Never trust the Tescire." He tossed it into the ocean.

"I knew that already. Come peacefully and it will be less painful for you," Andri said.

"If you get rid of me, you will only create a dozen more time bandits, only they will not live forever. There are many waiting in the wings to take my place." Pulling a capsule out of his waistband, Gabranth swallowed it before Andri could stop him. Convulsing, greenish foam burbled from Gabranth's mouth. Andri, Augustin, and Trevor watched helplessly. When the convulsions stopped, Gabranth lay dead.

"Poison," Andri said. A crowd gathered around. "Call the police, this man is dead," he yelled.

He felt Freyja at his elbow. "We should go. I sense bad men on the trail, coming this way."

He nodded at Augustin and Trevor and they slipped into the crowd. When they were out of sight of the beach, Augustin said, "Okay, Aladar, get us out of here."

They walked out of the seer pool together.

"The activities of the Tescire are hidden from me. Their whole planet is now shielded from my view. I'm going to stop missions for now, until their activities become clearer." Aladar said.

The men walked into the cafeteria, while Freyja headed to her room.

Andri stopped to talk to her. "Aren't you going to come tell tall tales of our latest adventure?"

Her lower lip trembled. "I killed two men and I watched another die a horrible death. I tried to be a brave

Viking girl." The trembling grew worse. She threw herself into his arms, "Oh, Andri!" She sobbed uncontrollably on his shoulder.

He held her tight until she stopped crying. "Are you all right?"

"I'm sorry, I got your shoulder all wet again." Shaking her head, she said, "I'm going to rest in my room for now. Don't tell the others I broke down." She didn't wait for an answer but walked in and closed the door behind her.

Andri set himself down at the table. "I don't understand women."

"And you never will," answered Augustin.

Trevor creased his forehead. "What do you mean? Are you talking about Freyja?"

Andri nodded. "One moment she's as tough as nails, the next she's fragile. I don't understand."

"She's been through a lot. She's still tough as nails in front of us. It just means she's trusting you if she shows you her fragile side."

Augustin elbowed Trevor. "Look at you, the woman expert."

"I've had girlfriends now and again through the centuries."

Augustin turned to Andri. "Trust me, don't try to understand them, it will just make you crazy. Look at Trevor here."

"Hey, watch it."

Later that night a quiet knock came on Andri's door. "Open," he said.

Freyja stood there with a red dress on, which complemented her complexion perfectly. Her hands were clasped in front of her and her shoulder hunched up.

"Well, come in." Andri said.

She slowly made her way in and sat on a chair across from him. "I didn't want to bother you."

"You're not bothering me in the least. How can I help?"

"You once said that you found out about the planets by reading books. I want to do that also."

"Sure, all you have to do is ask the computer and it will get you any book you want. You have a choice between electronic or paper. I'm from a backward planet so I prefer the paper ones, but Trevor only uses the electronic ones. They come in all the major languages of the galaxy and there are translation programs that can convert them to Icelandic, if you want. Which do you think you would prefer?"

She looked down at her toes, "Can you teach me to read?"

"Oh, um, yes of course."

Her eyes brightening, "Thank you so much!" She cleared her throat, "Please don't tell the others."

"Don't be silly. It isn't a bad thing you need to keep secret. They would be more than happy to help also."

"Really, do you think so?"

"Yes."

He pulled a book off the shelf. "This one is about your country. I read it after I went there to save you. It's about what happened to it after you left and how it's doing now. Do you know... I'm sorry, of course you don't, how could you? Anyway, they, to this day, don't have an army. They protect their fishing rights fiercely, and they use a lot of geothermal energy."

"Really? What happened to the Vikings?"

"Oh, they're still there, I mean their descendants anyway, but they don't go on raids. They live peaceful lives now.. They're still known to be great travelers."

"Great, let's start with that one, then."

"Sit next to me and I'll show you how to read."
After she moved, he said, "I've never taught anyone to read before. I guess we can start with the letters. See, this one's and A…"

Chapter Twenty-Nine

Andri stood by the seer pool. "Aladar, I want to see my mother."

"Oh, Andri, she's an old woman now."

"I don't care. I haven't seen her in a long time and now that we aren't doing missions, I have time."

"Okay, but I'm sending Freyja with you. She seems to sense evil. If someone is trying to hurt you, she'll feel them long before they get there."

"Okay, send for her. I'll wait."

Freyja entered the room of the seer pool. "I thought we weren't doing missions? I was reading a book."

"I'm going to see my mother. You're going to protect me," Andri replied.

"Oh, I see. Let's go." She took his hand. They stepped into the pool together.

The dusty streets that Andri remembered as a child stretched out before him. In the center of the town stood a large artillery piece, large enough to shoot into space. It was new to Andri.

"Are we in any danger?" Andri asked Freyja.

"No, I feel no ill intent."

He walked to the door of his childhood home and knocked. A frail voice called, "Come in."

Turning the handle, he entered. The house hadn't changed much from his childhood beyond new rugs on the floor. One of the paintings on the wall was different.

"Mom, it's me, Andri."

She sat up from her chair. Vacant eyes stared in his direction. "Andri! Come here."

When he was near enough to touch, she threw his arms around him. "I'm so glad you came. I'm going to call your father." She hit a button by his chair.

A few minutes later, he rushed into the room. His overalls were still dirty from working in the fields. "Oh, it's Andri." He hugged his son. "And Freyja is here, too."

"Freyja, you're such a sweet girl, come give me a hug." Freyja, wide-eyed, walked over and hugged Andri's mom and dad.

"How do you know Freyja?" Andri puzzled.

"When you came to warn us about the imminent Tescire invasion, the planet purchased long-range artillery pieces and put them in every city. Most of the Tescire's ships were destroyed before they could land. They retreated. Other planets adopted the same defenses. You saved us." His mother patted his arm.

He swallowed and looked over towards Freyja. She shook her head and shrugged.

"Let's get them something to eat." His mother said, her unseeing eyes staring in Andri's father's direction.

He nodded and went into the kitchen. Andri followed him, with Freyja in tow. "What's going on dad? How come mom isn't cooking? Did she say I saved you?"

His father gave him a half-hearted smile. "She's blind and the doctors say she's only got a week or two to live. She's had a good life; don't grieve for her."

Andri gasped. Freyja put her arm around him.

"As for the rest," his father continued. "Don't you remember you sneaked onto Tescire to find out what was going on with them, about ten years ago? You and Freyja discovered they were planning an attack on this planet to draw you out and capture you. You warned us, we stopped them. The governor of the planet decorated you himself."

"I see. We don't live in your timeline. To Freyja and me, it hasn't happened yet."

"Well, I hope it works out the same as before, then. We eat simple things now that I'm the cook. I hope you don't mind." He pulled out frozen dinners out and put them to heat. When the buzzer dinged, he set them on the table along with glasses of milk.

Andri's mother hobbled slowly into the kitchen.

"Honey," his father said. "You didn't have to come in here. I would have brought you some food."

"I want to eat at the table with my family," she said as she sat down.

He set the plates in front of them, "Okay, let's eat together."

Andri and Freyja spent the rest of the day there, catching up. As the evening shadows lengthened, his father took him aside. "Your mother grows tired, but she won't go to bed as long as you're here."

Andri nodded, "I will tell her goodbye then." Turning to her, he gave her a hug. "Freyja and I have to get back. It was great seeing you, Mom."

"Take care, my son."

As Andri and Freyja stepped out of the seer pool, Andri sat on the edge and buried his face in his hands. Freyja sat down beside him and rubbed his back. "I'm so sorry, Andri. I'm so sorry you're going through this. I watched them drown my mother. Your father loves your mother, I can see that. She's in good hands."

Andri took several deep breaths. "I haven't seen her in years, yet it still hurts." A tear slid down his cheek. He swiped it away. "I'm going to my room."

She nodded, "Of course," but he was already through the door at that point.

"I warned him not to go. She is old and frail. I knew it would break his heart," Aladar's voice murmured.

"Yes, but he learned something. He has to go to Tescire."

"Tescire? He can't go to Tescire. It's not safe there. I can't see Tescire. They've put that shield up."

Andri walked back into the room. He had an energy weapon strapped to his hip.

"Aladar doesn't want you to go," Freyja said.

He looked up, "Are you going to stop me?"

"I can't send you there. "They have the whole planet shielded against me," Aladar said.

"I'm going to my planet and taking a transport over to Tescire. They're an evil people. I have to stop them. They've hurt so many."

"How will I bring you back?"

"I'll figure that out later." Andri stepped into the pool. He didn't notice Freyja following him.

Chapter Thirty

"What are you doing here?" Andri noticed Freyja standing behind him.

"I'm coming with you."

"No, you're not. Aladar, take her back." He tapped his foot. "Aladar?"

Freyja scanned the area as if expecting to suddenly be back at the seer pool. She relaxed her shoulders. "See, I'm supposed to be here."

Andri's shoulders slumped. "Very well, let's go."

Instead of farmlands as far as the eye could see, there stood a large city around them with steel and concrete buildings. "Is this your planet?"

"Yes. This is the spaceport where everyone comes and goes from the planet."

"It looks totally different than when we visited your mom and dad."

"We won't be here long."

Andri marched up to a ticket office. "I need transport to Tescire."

The gray-haired man with a long mustache looked at Andri's beltline. "You can't take the weapon with you. Tescire has enough of those already. You can put it in a locker over there." The man pointed to a row of yellow lockboxes. "It'll be here when you get back."

"Sorry," Andri ran over and put it in a locker, then rushed back.

"I don't know why anyone would want to go to that evil planet anyway, but we do have daily transport there. Here are your tickets. That will be ten credits each."

Andri paid him.

"Gate eight," the ticket agent pointed to the corner.

Around the building, behind gate eight sat a small ship. Instead of the normal oval shape craft Andri was used to, it was long and flat on top and bottom, but rounded only on the sides.

"It's a rust bucket," Andri exclaimed.

"Tescire summers are very humid, hard on spacecraft." Andri turned to see a man in a blue coat and hat with three gold bars on his shoulders. He hit a button on the side of the ship and doors slid open. "Welcome aboard."

The inside was clean and furnished with leather chairs, paintings, and plush carpet. Andri and Freyja stepped in and sat down.

"I wasn't expecting to fly today, but Bob said I had customers. Tensions have risen with us and the Tescires lately. Nobody wants to go there." The captain shut the side door, then entered a passageway leading to the flight deck.

The engines on the side of the craft hummed to life. Freyja grabbed Andri's arm as they left the ground. "What's going on?"

"We're okay. To get to the other planet, we have to travel through space."

Wide-eyed, she swallowed, "Oh. I don't think I like this."

The ship went slow as it left the atmosphere, then rapidly gained speed.

Freyja white-knuckled the arms of her chair. "I'm sure of it, I don't like this."

Ten minutes later the captain came back in. Freyja's grip on the chair had relaxed by that time. "Anyone want breakfast? I'm starving."

"I would," Andri said.

Freyja looked at Andri, then the captain. "I haven't eaten in a while. I would like some food, too, please."

"Coming right up." He said as he opened up a cupboard on the side of the ship. Pulling out some eggs and other ingredients, he cooked up three omelets. He rolled in a table from the back of the craft and soon the three of them were eating breakfast complete with bacon, toast, and milk.

Andri looked around a minute later. "Who's flying this thing?"

The captain scooped up another fork full of eggs. "Autopilot. We'll be in Tescire in three days. All I need to do is land this ship when we're close. What is a Time God going to Tescire for, anyway?"

Andri blanched. "You recognize me?"

"Yep, it's real easy with the international traveler securities protocol. It scans all the passengers' faces and then I send the list ahead to Tescire so they know who's coming." He turned to Freyja, "You weren't in the database. No one has a record of you."

"We have to turn around. They can't know I'm coming. I have to go there without being known." Andri said.

The captain leaned back in his chair, "So you're on a mission. I thought as much. I haven't transmitted it. I have to the last day of our journey to do that. Then they will tell me yea or nay on whether you can disembark.

Incognito costs extra. I'll have to break all sorts of intergalactic laws."

"You can sneak us on the planet?" Andri asked, hopeful.

"Yes, I have a friend who you can trust. I'll signal him. His ship will match our speed and latch on to my ship and I'll transfer you over. He can hide his movements from the authorities because his ship is so well insulated. I'll send him a signal."

The captain went back into the flight deck and made the call. He was back soon. "He'll be ready before we're a day out."

"Thank you for doing that," Andri picked up his fork.

Two days later, Andri and Freyja heard a thump on the top of the spaceship.

"He's here," the captain said. Soon a hatch opened up above their heads and a man with black hair, an oil smear on his face, and faded blue coveralls stepped down a ladder.

"Karl, it's good to see you."

Karl, silent, nodded at the captain. He turned and touched a few buttons on the control panel.

"What are you doing?" the captain asked.

"You forgot to delete their profiles. I'm doing it for you."

"Oh, ya, um, that."

"Yes, that." He gazed over at Andri and Freyja. "We have to leave now."

The two of them rushed up the ladder followed by Karl. The hatch closed and the ships separated. Karl's ship was tiny in comparison to the one they just left. It had a bench in the back and a seat in front of the controls.

Karl turned sharply and headed towards the planet. "He didn't forget to delete the profiles. He was going to turn you in for the reward. Two hundred units is the highest reward I've ever seen for anybody. I make my money by smuggling people onto the planet, not by getting them caught. The last two I smuggled didn't make it two miles before they were caught. He's reporting them."

"What are you going to do?" Andri asked.

"I've got a new spot to land he doesn't know about. They will know you're on the planet but will have no idea where you are."

Freyja scooted over to Andri. "I'm scared, hold me." He put his arm around her and she snuggled closer.

Chapter Thirty-One

The spacecraft hit with a thud on the top of a two-story building. Karl shrugged. "Landings aren't my strong suit. You need to move quick. It won't take long for the authorities to realize there has been an unauthorized landing in a no landing zone. There's a hovercar at the base of the stairs. Please, try not to scratch the paint." He threw Andri the keys. "They know you're here, but not where; they will be looking for you. Her, they know nothing about."

Andri grabbed Freyja's hand and ran out of the open hatch, through the door on the top of the building and down the steps. He paused in front of the hovercar before helping Freyja in. "This is a nice hovercar. It even has extras." He pulled an energy weapon from between the seats. They headed out of town.

"What are we looking for?" Freyja asked.

"Something out of place. We found it, according to my parents. I want to find it again."

They drove around the area for hours, watching the comings and goings of troops and driving past military bases.

"They have a huge army," Freyja commented.

"Half of the male children are required to be in their army and women are expected to have many young. They are trying to take over the galaxy. Three planets, ill-prepared for war, were taken over by them. A lot more were attacked, but defeated them, including my homeworld."

"What terrible people."

"Yes, angry and unhappy."

"I'm hungry," Freyja complained.

"We could get something to eat. I'll pull over at the next place I see." He found a restaurant a mile away. He pulled over and started to get out.

"No, you're a wanted man. I'll go in and make sure the coast is clear."

"You're right. I need to stay out here. Here's the card, buy something and bring it back. We can eat in here." As she left, Andri darkened the windows on the hovercar and sat back to await her return.

Immediately, Freyja noticed the clientele was all male. Feeling uneasy, she turned to leave.

A large arm across the doorway blocked her escape. "What's the rush, cutie?"

Two men from the bar approached, "Turn on some music, Lorina, I suddenly have a dance partner." As the man went to grab her arm, she bit him. "My, my, I do like it when they play hard to get." He stepped forward again, but suddenly doubled over.

Andri stood next to Freyja, his right hand clenched in a fist and the left hand held the pistol. "Leave her alone." He grabbed Freyja's hand and led her out of the place. No one tried to stop them.

They hopped in the car and drove quickly away.

"What was that place?" Freyja asked.

"I guess I don't know enough about this planet. I haven't read that much about it, but it seems that only the men go out to eat, and not the women." He scanned the road behind them. "We're being followed."

She turned. "There are a lot of them. What can we do?"

"Hang on." He sped up and took the corner sharp, then the next corner, zigzagging through town. At last, he doubled back and parked in a blind alley. Three other hovercars sped by.

"Did you lose them?" she asked.

"I'm going to stay here a minute more, just in case."

A few minutes later, a police car, with lights and siren on, blew past.

"That's not good. I'm heading to the next town." He pulled out, heading in the opposite direction. After a couple of miles, he suddenly stopped.

"What is it?" Freyja asked.

A spacecraft slowly landed in a fenced-in field next to thousands of identical craft. "Flybus. It's my home's planetary transportation system. What are the buses doing here? I didn't know they had so many of them." He stared for a minute. Soldiers marched into one of the buses. "Wait. That's how they're going to invade. They are putting their soldiers in buses that my people won't suspect. When they land, instead of our own people getting off, it will be hoards of the enemy. I've got to warn my people."

"How do we get off this planet?"

"I don't know. Go back to the house and contact Karl, I guess."

Freyja looked at the tower, "What's that?"

Andri slowed as he gazed up at it. "It's their interplanetary shield. That's why Aladar couldn't move us on or off this planet. They have her blocked."

"Can't we get Aladar to bring us back if the shield isn't up?"

A small explosion shook the car. Smoke filled the inside. Andri grabbed the gun and pulled Freyja to him. Exiting the car, energy bolts flashed past him. Four police cars had him boxed in. With Freyja over his shoulder, he blasted a hole in the fence. Looking up at the tower, he saw a blue haze emitting from it. He turned just in time to see two policemen trying to get through the hole in the fence. Two energy blasts and they ducked down. *How do I disable this tower?* A large conduit led up into the tower. *I cut the power.* He shot the conduit. Sparks flew everywhere. Flames burst out, and the blue haze stopped coming out of the top of the tower. *I hope that worked.* "Aladar, now would be a good time to get us out of here."

Andri walked out of the seer pool with Freyja still over his shoulder. He set her down on the ground in front of it.

"Is she okay?" Aladar asked.

"She's still breathing."

Freyja coughed, so Andri rolled her over to her side. She coughed a couple more times. Augustin rushed in. "What happened?"

"They started shooting at us. I don't think she was hit."

"Smoke? Was there a lot of smoke?"

"Yes, inside the hovercar. The windshield was smashed on my side, but her side was intact."

"I've got just the thing," Augustin ran back down the hall. Trevor and five others came into the seer pool room.

When Augustin burst back through, he yelled, "Make room." The crowd parted and let him through. "Help me sit her up."

Andri and he leaned her against the wall. Augustin poured a white liquid slowly down her throat. She choked. In a few minutes her color returned to normal and she drew in a large breath.

Augustin sat against the seer pool. Wiping his forehead, he said, "She'll be all right."

Andri and Augustin walked her down the hall into the infirmary. Laying her on the bed, Augustin put monitors on her. "I can't wait to hear the story of this one. We'll have to wait till she gets better though."

"I can tell you the story," Andri said.

Augustin shook his head, "It wouldn't be the same."

Chapter Thirty-Two

Freya sat in the cafeteria in her bathrobe. She seemed to be recovering nicely, but all the men were keeping an eye on her. They sat around her in a group listening to the telling of her and Andri's latest adventure. Andri sat a few seats down eating his soup.

"Why don't you join the group?" Andri looked up to see Trevor standing over him.

"I know this story."

"Yes, but she tells it so well."

Andri sighed. "Is she telling the part where I almost lost her? I was looking at the tower and not paying attention to what was going on around me."

"You saved her, dragged her to safety. In her eyes, you're a hero."

"I don't feel much like a hero. I've got to go and stop an invasion anyway." Andri walked down the hall and changed clothes. When he arrived at the seer pool, Freyja was waiting for him.

"You can't come this time," Andri said.

"According to your mother, I was there. I'm going with you."

He held out his hand. "Fine, we can take it easy this time, come on."

She smiled and took his hand.

"Mom," Andri called as he neared the house. She ran out and hugged him.

"Andri, it's so good to see you and you brought a friend."

"Mom, this is Freyja."

"It's so good to see you," she hugged Freyja too. "I always hoped that Andri would find someone."

Freyja blushed.

"It's not like that, Mom."

His mother smirked. "Come in, come in."

"Can you look after Freyja for a minute? She was recently hurt. I have to warn the council of an impending invasion."

"Of course, dear." She put her arm around Freyja and led her into the house. "Tell me all about it."

Andri ran to the law room. The guards stood aside and let him in. The delegates were in a discussion when he walked up. It ended immediately.

"Andri, come forward." Rel Li motioned to him.

"The Tescire are going to invade. They are disguising their landing craft as Flybus ships. They will be on the ground before we have a chance to stop them." Andri didn't realize how out of breath he was until that moment.

The room erupted in chatter. Rel Li held up his hands. "I want you to warn your people. We will have cannons set up in every city and town. I hereby ground the Flybus fleet. If anything tries to land after today, in anything that looks like a Flybus ship, we will blast it."

Rel Li patted Andri on the back. "You said you would help us, and you did. The whole planet thanks you."

Andri rushed back to his parent's place. When he walked in, his mother and father, all of his father's farm hands, some of the neighbors, and a few people Andri didn't know, were all gathered around listening to Freyja's stories.

"Sorry to interrupt. I have to get Freyja home. She was recently wounded and hasn't completely healed yet."

The crowd all looked up at him, realizing for the first time, he was standing there.

One lady hugged him. "We didn't realize what brave and amazing things you were doing around the galaxy."

June, the neighbor lady smiled at him, "Your girlfriend is such a delight."

Freyja stood up and slipped her hand in his. "I have to go, but it was nice meeting all of you."

"Don't you want to wait and see what happens with the invasion and all?" Andri's mother asked.

"I've already seen the future. You destroy the enemy before they land. It's a complete victory," Andri answered. *Then you die ten years after that.* He looked at the ground.

"Oh, good." She hugged him again. "Take care, son. It was so nice meeting you, Freyja. I hope you to get feeling better."

As they stepped out of the seer pool, Freyja leaned against him. "I'm so tired."

He put his arm around her and led her to her room. Laying her down in the bed, he said, "Don't get up until you feel better."

She nodded and fell asleep even before he made it out of her quarters.

"Andri, I have a mission for you." Aladar's voice awakened him from a deep sleep.

"I'm on my way." He dressed and went down to the seer pool. To his surprise, all the other travelers were there. "What's going on?"

Augustin answered, "It's your last mission as an apprentice Time God. We all wanted to give you a warm send off. Be warned; this will be your toughest mission yet."

Andri swallowed as he looked at the others. His gaze stopped at Freyja. She had on her bath robe. Her eyes were red.

"I'm so scared for you," she said as she threw her arms around him. "I asked Aladar to let me go with you. She said you would have to do this one on your own."

"I'll be fine, this isn't my first mission."

"Yes, but they said it would be the most dangerous."

He swallowed as he stepped into the seer pool. *What have I gotten myself into?*

Chapter Thirty-Three

Explosions thundered over his head. Andri hit the ground. Dead men lay on either side of him, some dressed in blue uniforms, others in red. Another explosion caused Andri to duck again. Gunfire erupted to his right. Getting to his knees, Andri scanned the area. He ducked back down as bullets whizzed by his head. Someone fell to the ground next to him. He looked up to see a young boy with a drum getting back to his feet.

"Hot work today." Just then the drum he carried shattered. The boy fell backwards to the ground.

"Are you all right?"

A sob came out, "My drum."

"You're bleeding." The white pants to his uniform turned red at the boy's hip.

"I'm okay, but my drum." He stood up but found his right leg wouldn't support him. "I think I'm not so good after all."

Andri ripped the trousers where the bullet entered. Having passed through the drum first, the ball wasn't deep under the skin. Searching the area, he found a bayonet and took it off on one of the dead soldiers. "This is going to hurt. Bite down on your drum strap."

The drummer did as he was told. Getting under the ball, Andri was able to dislodge it. He ignored the groanings of the boy. Andri tore off his own sleeve and bound it around the man's waist. "There that will have to do. I'm taking you to the rear."

"No," the drummer boy had spit out the strap and was shaking his head violently. "We need to report to the commander."

"Fine, where is he?" Before Andri even finished the question, a hand was pointing in the direction of a group of men. "Here, I'll help you to your feet. I'm Andri, what's your name?"

"Joseph."

The two of them went limping back to the tent of Joseph's commander. Situated behind a long ditch, it sat out of reach from the guns from the town.

"Who are you?" snapped the commander.

"I'm Andri. I brought back your wounded man."

"Whose army are you in?"

"I'm not in the army. I was caught in the middle of this, and found this wounded man, so I brought him to you."

"You're in my army now. Put on that uniform." The officer pointed to a coat with a bullet hole near the heart. Blood stained the outside of it. "I'm going to need every man I can get for the morning attack."

Taking off his shirt, Andri put on the uniform. He dabbed the blood off as best that he could. *I saved the drummer boy, so why am I still here?* He knew better than ask it out loud. If he did, Aladar would fuss at him when he arrived back at the seer pool. He slid down in the trench and awaited his fate.

The ground shook as the cannons behind Andri opened up on the enemy. He sat straight up from a deep sleep.

"The carol of the cannons," a dirty man sitting next to him said.

"Oh," Andri went to stand up, but the man dragged him back down.

"That's Reggie's uniform you have on. You don't want to end up like he did. Stay down."

Andri sat back down.

"Charles is my name What's yours?"

"Andri."

"Well, young Andri, we'll be going against redoubt ten. That's what they call it anyway. If you peek over the edge of the trench, you'll see it next to the water."

Andri crawled up the edge of the trench. The structure consisted of dirt piled up, with sharpened logs poking out of it to stop troops from rushing to the top. "I don't even know where I am."

"That's Yorktown in the background. We have Cornwallis cornered there. Fix your bayonet, here we go. Hamilton's signaling us forward."

Andri climbed out of the trench and rushed forward with the rest of the troops.

"Who goes there?" a sentry called out. He fired when no one answered. Soon the whole redoubt fired down on them. Fighting erupted to Andri's left at another redoubt. He slid through the hole his fellow soldiers had cut through the spiked wood logs. With great effort, he rushed past the dead and wounded men to the top of the embankment. When he arrived, the battle was already over. British and German troops were either running towards Yorktown or surrendering.

Joseph stood on top of the redoubt, facing the enemy and playing his new drum.

"Shore up the defenses, they'll want their redoubts back for sure."

Andri looked up to see an officer pointing with his sword. He followed several fellow soldiers to the back of the redoubt and piled dirt and rocks on top of the wall.

Behind him, in the distance, Andri saw men and horses bringing up cannons.

Charles handed Andri a shovel. "This will work better than that bayonet of yours."

"Thank you."

When the newly moved cannons opened up, Andri saw the shells hitting the town itself.

"Nowhere for them to hide now," Charles replied. He handed Andri some tobacco. "Here, have a chaw."

"No, thank you."

"Smart boy, it's a nasty habit. The wife hates it. You got a girl, young Andri?"

Andri sat down and stared into the distance. "Two."

"Two? How do you keep them from finding out about each other?"

"They're not from the same pla…, um area."

"A girl in every town. Ah, to be young again."

Andri smiled, "It's not like that. One has moved on with her life and it doesn't include me. The other I get to see every day."

"Is she nearby then?"

"I mean, when I'm home, I see her every day."

"Ah. Do you want something to eat? I've got some hardtack. It's not too maggoty."

"No, I'm good for now."

"Get down," Charles warned. Soon shells were landing all around them. A whistling sound, then the ground shook as the shell exploded. When the bombardment let up, Charles stood up and brushed himself off. "They are not happy with us over there in Yorktown."

Chapter Thirty-Four

Andri woke up starving. He had been there two days, and had even eaten the hardtack. His ears rang constantly as shells from the guns behind him bombarding the town. Then there were the less frequent British shells aimed at the redoubt.

The sun peeked over the smoke-filled horizon.

"They're up to no good. Load your gun and get ready, young Andri."

"I don't know how." *Energy weapons are so much easier. Point and shoot.*

"You aren't a soldier, are you? Here," Charles poured gunpowder down the barrel with his powder horn. "Then you ram the ball down there. Once you prime it, you're all set."

"Thanks."

"Here they come."

Andri could just make out the shapes moving towards their position in the early light. Shots rang out. He aimed and fired. The dark shape crumpled and fell. *I'm supposed to be helping the people of this planet, not killing them.* Andri swallowed hard as he loaded his gun again and took aim. The enemy turned to retreat. He held his fire.

"They won't be back soon. We taught them a lesson today."

"What about their wounded? We can't just leave them there," Andri said.

"They'll shoot anyone that leaves the redoubt. No, we stay here."

Andri watched as some of the British soldiers crawled back towards their own lines. Others moaned. After an hour or two, the moaning would stop.

A firefight broke out in the distance. Andri watched it with morbid fascination. Smoke rose from both sides as they fired their muskets.

Andri turned to see Charles peering over the edge beside him. "They don't like the trap we set for them. They're trying to leave."

"Did they make it?"

Charles gazed over. "No, they're retreating."

"What now?"

"We wait to see what Mr. Cornwallis does. He's trapped."

Andri slid back down into the fortification. *Why am I still here? I'm hungry, I'm cold, and I'm not accomplishing anything.*

Charles shook Andri awake. "It's a flag, a white flag. They're surrendering."

Andri clamored up to the top of the wall. There, flying above Yorktown, was a large white flag.

Cheers rose up from the men. He could hear cheers rising from the other redoubts and cannon crews.

Three days later, they stood at attention as the enemy passed by. They laid down their weapons and were marched off. Their band played as they passed by.

Andri whispered to Charles, "What song is that?"

"The world turned upside down."

"Oh."

The men were allowed to wash their uniforms and were fed some real food for the first time in days. Andri sat in a tent enjoying a full stomach and feeling clean, when a man beckoned him out.

Charles stood next to him. "This is the lad I was telling you about, Sir."

"Andri, I'm Alexander Hamilton. I want you to deliver this message to Philadelphia." He handed Andri an envelope.

Andri looked over at Charles. "Where's Philadelphia?"

"I'd better go with you lad. I'll get passes from the commander."

A few minutes, he came back. "I have the passes and two horses. You do know how to ride a horse?"

Andri nodded. His dad had horses on the family farm.

They took off towards Philadelphia a few minutes later. Riding through the countryside, no one bothered them. They rode fast, only stopping to water the horses. On one of these stops, Andri saw men moving around in the woods. He handed Hamilton's letter to Charles.

Two muskets poked out between the trees, "Halt, who goes there?"

Andri saw the red uniforms. He had been standing, but Charles had mounted his horse. He slapped the back of Charles' horse. "Ride like the wind." Andri knocked down the barrel of the muskets. The shots went harmlessly in the ground. A pistol went off. Andri felt a sting in his shoulder. He grabbed it as two men knocked him to the ground. A British officer stood over him. "What was your mission?"

Andri grimaced in pain, but he refused to speak.

"Get him," the officer said. "We'll make him talk."

"Aladar, now would be a good time."

One of the men hit him in the gut with the butt of his rifle. "Quiet."

They dragged him through the woods. A few yards later he was set down in front of another officer's tent. The man came out. He sported a bright red uniform with all sorts of decorations on it. "What have we here?"

"A messenger, Sir. He handed over an envelope right before we captured him. The other man got away."

The officer pulled a bayonet off one of the men's guns. He jabbed it into the musket ball wound in Andri's shoulder. Andri screamed.

"I don't have time to ask you politely. What did the message say?"

"I don't know. I didn't read it."

He poked it into the wound again. Andri screamed in pain. "What do you think it said? Who sent it? Where was it going to and from?"

Shaking, Andri looked for somewhere to throw up. "Hamilton sent it. I don't know what he said. Probably telling about the surrender of Cornwallis at Yorktown."

"You lie! Cornwallis would never surrender." The officer backhanded Andri in the face. "Throw him on a horse. We're leaving here."

They packed up the tent and were on the road in an hour. A warship stood off the coast. The horses rode up to the shore. They put Andri in a boat and rowed him to the ship, then set him down on the deck, where an officer in a blue uniform stood over him. He looked over at the commander who'd jabbed Andri with the bayonet. "Why hasn't his wound been attended to?"

"He's a rebel. He lies. He says that Cornwallis has surrendered."

"He's not lying. Cornwallis has surrendered. Go get the surgeon."

"What?"

The naval officer's face reddened. "I said, go get the surgeon."

The man hurried off.

The officer sat down next to Andri. "We're not barbarians. This war will be over soon. I can't see throwing you in a prison ship to rot and die."

A man with a blood-stained apron came up with his bag in hand. He took one look at Andri's shoulder and said, "Bite down on this." He shoved a leather strap in Andri's mouth. He turned to the two sailors nearby. "Hold down his arms."

Taking a hook out of his bag, he dug into the wound. Andri tried to scream. He bit down hard on the leather.

A small lead ball came out and rolled down the deck. The surgeon stitched up the wound, then bandaged it. "There, should be fine." He packed up his bag, pulled the leather strap out of Andri's mouth and left.

"Set this man to shore and let him go," the officer commanded.

Andri watched the ship sail away from the shoreline, wondering what this mission had been all about.

Chapter Thirty-Five

When he heard an approaching horse, Andri hid in the woods.

"Andri, lad, where are you?"

Andri stepped out. "Charles?"

"There you are. I thought they were going to take you back to England with them for a minute. When I saw you coming back, my heart leapt with joy."

"I thought you'd be almost to Philadelphia by now."

"No, not without you." He handed the envelope back to Andri. "'Charles,' I said to myself, 'We're going together, even if it means going by way of England to get there.'"

Andri laughed, then gritted his teeth as he held his shoulder.

"Does it hurt much?"

"Only when I laugh." He thought for a minute. "Or talk, or walk, or breathe."

"Let's get going. We have work to do."

Andri climbed up on the horse and the two of them rode on, day and night.

"You have brought us wonderful news." Andri had been surprised to be at the address of a newspaper instead of a military base or politician. The man behind the desk smiled and wrote a note back to Hamilton. "Here, take this with you, when you return."

Return? Andri hadn't thought about that. He smiled through gritted teeth, "Yes, Sir."

Outside Charles was waiting with the horses. "Well?"

"Our message was a newspaper article. The editor wants us to bring this note back to Hamilton."

Charles grabbed the note. "I'll take that. You didn't sign up for this. Ditch the uniform and go home. I'll tell Hamilton you were captured by the British, which is true. The war will be over soon anyway."

"Thank you." Andri could have argued, but he so wanted to be done with this mission. His shoulder hurt. Augustin would have some type of pain reliever in his bag of tricks.

Without another word, Charles rode off with the other horse in tow.

Andri took a few steps, looked both directions then said, "Can I come home now, Aladar?"

He was so relieved to be stepping out of the seer pool. All the other travelers were there waiting for him. Freyja rushed over and hugged him.

"The shoulder, watch the shoulder."

"Sorry." She stepped back.

"You did well, Andri. Washington will become the president, Hamilton will have praises heaped upon him for his attack on the redoubt, Charles will become a Senator, and Joseph will become of mayor of a major city. None of them will ever forget you and what you did for their country." He could hear the happiness in Aladar's voice.

"What about the man I killed?" Andri asked.

"You hit him in the belt buckle. He doubled over in pain, but he had only a large bruise. You didn't kill anyone."

Andri sighed softly.

"Let me look at that shoulder of yours," Augustin said. When Andri peeled back the soiled bandage, the smell almost knocked him over. "It's hot to the touch. That captain said he wasn't a barbarian, but that surgeon sure was. I'll fix it up for you." They walked back to Andri's quarters. Augustin ran and grabbed his medical bag.

Injecting the wound, Augustin deadened the pain then took out the stitches. Scrubbing out the wound to get rid of the infection, he put white powder on it, then stitched it back up, "Properly, this time." He gave Andri a pill. "Take this and plan on sleeping for the next ten to twelve hours."

Andri nodded, swallowed the pill and was out like a light.

He woke up to find Freyja sitting by his bedside. "Um, hi."

"I was so worried. I sat there and watched in the seer pool the whole time you were gone. I heard every word you said."

His eyebrows raised, "Every word?"

"Yes, I especially liked the part where you see your girl every day. I'm the only one you see every day." She leaned down and kissed him. Keeping her face just inches from his, she went on, "I'm supposed to bring you to the great hall when you wake."

"Yes, let's go right away." The situation was getting uncomfortable; a distraction was what was needed.

They went hand in hand past the seer pool and up the tunnel that led to the Temple of the Rock.

Andri hadn't been there since the first day he'd become a traveler. A door he'd never seen before stood open. Lit by torches, it was lined with keepers of the stone in their red robes holding their toc'fi. At the end of the long room were all the Time Gods with Aladar at their head. On the altar lay a golden scepter.

"Come forward, Andri." Aladar motioned to him.

When he stood in front of her, she beckoned him to kneel before the altar. Picking up the scepter, she touched both shoulders with it.

"Ouch," he said when she touched the wounded one.

"Sorry." She lay the scepter back on the altar. "When you came to us, you were our apprentice. Now you have qualified to be a full-fledged Time God. You may stand."

When he did, the other Time Gods cheered him.

She continued, "Look upon the walls."

He gazed around, there were nine pictures of men adorning the walls.

"This is the hall of heroes. These are the Time Gods who died protecting the galaxy. Every Time God owes a debt of gratitude to these men. We will have a moment of silence for them."

Everyone bowed their heads.

Aladar, and the keepers marched back up to the Temple of the Rock.

"Come, I have the feast ready," Dorik said.

All the Time Gods marched down to the cafeteria. There, spread out on the tables, was an array of the galaxy's finest foods.

"Well, you made it. I didn't think you were going to make it through the last mission. Luckily you did it. Now you can go on the real missions. You've only had easy ones up to this point. Something to cut your teeth on," Trevor explained.

"Real missions?" Andri swallowed. " You mean, they get harder?"

"Oh, yes. Much harder."

Freyja walked up to Andri and put her arm around him. "You really should try some of that Balterian Boar, it's delicious." As she caught his gaze she asked, "Is your shoulder hurting? Your face is so pale all of a sudden."

The End

See Sample Chapter of A Witch's Revenge at the end of this book

Other Books by Clark Graham

Time Loop Series

A Loop in Time
A Hole in Time
A Rift in Time

Galactic War Series

End of the Innocent
The Last War

Elvenshore Series

Dwarves of Elvenshore
The Lost Cities of Elvenshore
Elf's Bane
The Last of the Minotaur
Curse of the Druid King
War of the Druid King
Dwarves Druids and Dragons
Return of the Druid

Wizard Series

Wizards and Heroes
Trouble With Dragons

Other Books

A Witch's Revenge
Bullets and Blondes
Children of the Gods
Emily and the Shadow King
International Mysteries
Millennium Man
Moon Over Mykonos
Murder Beneath the Palms
Nick Spool: Galactic Private Eye (Free)
Return of the Druid
State Secrets

Sample Chapter

A Witch's Revenge

Chapter 1

A flash of lightning brightened the dark room like a spotlight slashing across the sky. A few seconds later, a deep rumble shook the whole house. A frail silvery-haired woman gazed out upon the storm. A knitted blue shawl hung loosely from her thin shoulders.

"That was close." Her quiet voice was soon lost to the sound of the rain crashing down.

"Joan, get back away from that window." Sitting in a rocking chair, the other woman knitted. A basket of yarn sat on the floor next to her. She rocked gently back and forth, barely looking up as the room lit up suddenly again.

"Why, Momma…" The rest of her words were drowned out by a thunderous boom.

"That's why. Lightning isn't afraid of a little glass."

Joan cleared her throat. "Well, I'm not afraid of it, either." Her shoulders flinched at the next blast. Sound and light struck at the same time. It shook the windows violently, but they held. The rain intensified, and soon all Joan could see was water cascading down the glass. She stepped back and sat down on the faded sofa.

"It's directly over the house now. That's not a good sign." Momma continued her knitting.

"Is tonight the night?"

Momma looked up, eyes round with sympathy. "We can't think like that."

Jim Taylor looked out upon the same storm. Candles lit the inside of his home. The flames danced, casting eerie shadows around the room. His fence swayed in the wind as he watched and worried. His thought of running out and bracing it was quelled by the sudden deluge of water coming from the clouds. He sighed heavily.

Another bolt lit up the yard. There, just outside the window, stood a young woman. "Huh?" He stared harder but couldn't see her now through the darkness. Lightning lit the yard up again. The woman stood there, wet and nude.

He grabbed his overcoat and headed outside. "What are you doing?" He threw the coat over her. "Come inside, you're going to catch your death of cold out there." He guided her into the house. She offered no resistance.

He sat her down on a chair in the kitchen. "What's your name? What are you doing in my yard?"

Gentle eyes stared at him, but not a sound left her lips. Her brown shoulder-length hair dripped.

He dried off his face with a dishtowel from the drawer, then handed her one. She took it, but set it in her lap and didn't dry off with it.

Hating his wet, clingy clothes, he ran up the stairs and changed into a dry t-shirt. Coming back down, he dialed the sheriff. "Bob, is there a missing person's report on a young woman? She doesn't talk, at least she hasn't yet. Can you come out and get her?"

"I've got a thousand people without power up and down the county. There are lines down and it's all we can do to keep up with the real emergencies. Jim, you can handle a girl for a few hours, right? Feed her something." The phone went dead.

"Feed her something," he mumbled under his breath. "No way to cook it with the power out."

Grabbing cold cereal out of the cupboard, he poured it into a bowl along with some milk. Putting a spoon in it, he handed it to the girl. She stared down at the food.

He grabbed a bowl of his own. "You do this." He picked up a spoonful and stuffed it into his mouth. She cocked her head sideways as she watched him.

"You do it." She didn't move. "Okay, I get it. Not a cereal eater." He reached for her bowl.

She shrieked and moved it out of his reach.

"Sorry." He pulled back his hand. "I thought you didn't want it."

Watching him suspiciously, she took a spoonful and tasted it. Without a change of expression, she stuffed more in her mouth. Soon, the bowl was empty. She sat it in her lap.

"Do you want some more?"

Her expression didn't change.

"More?" He mimicked putting a spoon in his mouth.

Again, no response.

He reached slowly for the bowl. This time she let him take it. After putting the bowl in the sink, he grabbed a blanket out of the closet. Leading her over to the couch, he pointed. "You can sleep here."

Before he could blink, she took off the overcoat, revealing her pale skin, and laid down. She pulled the blanket over herself and was soon sound asleep.

He shrugged. Sleep sounded like a good idea, so he headed upstairs.

Made in the USA
Lexington, KY
24 November 2019